DRAGON BAY

Violet Winspear

Lucan Savidge was virtually a stranger to Kara when she married him, distraught as she was with unhappiness over the end of her love affair with the sweetheart of her youth—but the step was taken, and now it was too late to turn back. It was her arrival at Dragon Bay, the home of the Savidge family, that brought the truth so overwhelmingly to Kara. They were all hard, bitter, unable, it seemed, to love. Just what kind of a marriage had Kara made?

DRAGON BAY

Violet Winspear

Curley Publishing, Inc.
South Yarmouth, Ma.

Library of Congress Cataloging-in-Publication Data

Winspear, Violet.
   Dragon Bay / Violet Winspear.
      p.   cm.
   1. Large type books.   I. Title.
[PR6073.I5543D7   1990]
823'.914—dc20
ISBN 0–7927–0159–3 (lg. print)   89–23771
                                                    CIP

© **Violet Winspear 1969**

Published in Large Print by arrangement with Harlequin Enterprises B.V.

Printed in Great Britain

DRAGON BAY

CHAPTER ONE

A TRIM yacht flying a Greek flag put into harbour at Fort Fernand, and some time later one of her passengers came ashore, followed by a sailor carrying a couple of suitcases.

The alighting girl was about twenty-one, slim, almost boyish, clad in a blue reefer jacket over beige slacks, with a jaunty cap perched on her long dark hair. Her eyes beneath the peak of her cap were deep and dark as peaty pools, and tiny gold rings glinted in the lobes of her ears.

'That looks like a hotel.' She spoke in Greek to the sailor and gestured at a building with ornamental balconies, batwing shutters, and red-flowering palms in its courtyard. 'I will put up there for a few days,' she added, and gazed around at her tropical surroundings. The sails of sloops and schooners bobbed in the harbour, and from out of salt and sun-faded sheds came a strong smell of fish, and tobacco in storage.

Poinsettias flowered gaudy and large against white walls, and the patches of welcome shadow were ebony dark as the Carib eyes of an old man who sat smoking a pipe on the cobbled wall of the waterfront. The girl met his gaze, and it came home forcibly to her that she was now in the French Caribbean and far from her own Greek shores.

When she and the sailor reached the hotel, he carried in her suitcases and she bade him goodbye in Greek. '*Adio*,' she said. 'Tell my brother that I have chosen the Isle de Luc for my—holiday, and I hope to be home in time to celebrate my darling nephew's third birthday.'

The sailor flashed her a smile, for having been long employed by the Stephanos family, he knew the strength of the affection between Paul Stephanos and his slip of a sister. Even now Kara was a woman, she was still so young to look at, with her enormous Greek eyes holding that hint of sadness and gaiety that made her almost lovely when she smiled, or held young Dominic in her arms.

'*Adio*, Miss Kara.' The sailor gave her a smart salute. 'I hope you have a happy holiday.'

Happy holiday? She smiled briefly and bleakly as she approached the reception desk of the Hotel Victoire and pinged the bell on the counter. It echoed through the siesta quiet, broken only by the whirring of ceiling fans, and then a corpulent Creole came

2

shambling out of a room at the back of the counter, his sleepy, disgruntled face creasing in smiles that matched the creases in the white jacket he was pulling on.

Yes, they had accommodation for her. This was not yet the tourist season and the hotel was half empty. He swung the register towards her, and his eyes chased over her as she took up the pen to sign her name. She noticed the singularity of the name on the line above hers—Lucan Savidge, resident of Dragon Bay, Isle de Luc.

She gave a slight laugh. What a savage name and address, both of which probably belonged to a man as meek as a mouse!

The bell pinged again, and a coloured boy emerged from the shade of a potted palm and came to carry her suitcases to the iron-caged lift. Her room was situated on the second floor, midway along the corridor. It was quite spacious, with a wrought-iron balcony overlooking the patio of the hotel, and furniture, she was sure, from the Colonial days.

The boy told her in lisping Creole that the bathroom was at the end of the corridor, and that there would be no hot water for a bath until later that evening. 'It has a shower, *mam'zelle.*' His smile was sugar-white. 'Ver' cool, we here at Hotel Victoire. Up to date for

3

tourists—you tourist?'

'I suppose you could say that.' Her French had been learned at school and the boy looked puzzled, then pleased by the size of his tip.

'You want a guide, I take you all over town, show you the sights,' he offered.

'Perhaps,' she ushered him out of the room. 'What do I call you, in case I want to see the sights?'

He cocked his head, alert and impish. 'Napoleon my name,' he grinned. 'Nap for short.'

'Very well, Nap for short.' Kara grinned back at the boy, for she had the rare gift of being able to adjust to the ages of the young and the old. 'If I want you, I'll whistle.'

'Okay,' he said, and was gone like a dark shadow along the corridor, its windows shuttered against the hot afternoon sunshine. Kara closed the door of her room and tossed off her nautical cap and jacket. She ran her fingers through her long hair, slightly rough from the sea-water and sun she never avoided. Kara sighed. The girl Nikos had married in America was golden-haired, pale-skinned, beautiful and pampered.

The locks of her suitcase clicked loud in the room as she opened it and began to unpack. She shook out the linen dress she would wear

4

that evening and hung it over the hard back of a Colonial chair. She tossed wisps of nylon to the foot of the net-draped bed, and then her fingers clenched on a leather frame and she stood for a long moment gazing at the photograph of her brother Paul, an arm firmly locked about the slender waist of his wife, Domini. Beside them on the parapet of a terrace sat a small, lively-eyed boy, and Paul's other arm was holding him with equal firmness.

Kara smiled even as a band of pain seemed to clasp her throat. Her own dear Apollo, who had fought the darkness that had almost taken his life and found so bright a love.

Domini, to whom Kara had taken her aching heart after receiving the letter that had shattered her own dream of a love and a life like her sister-in-law's. Like a broken song, the letter would not release her from its words, still they haunted her.

Sweet Kara,
   You will forgive and understand, I know. We made a pledge and said we would marry each other, but we did not take into account the sudden love for a stranger, from a stranger, that can come along and change all our youthful plans.

5

I am married, little Greek friend. Her name is Cicely and we met soon after I came here to Boston to run our shipping business in this part of the world. I am very much in love. I know it is the love that a man feels only once in a lifetime.

You too, Kara, will find love as I have found it, and then you will be as happy as I am. . . .

Happy . . . without Nikki? The companion of most of her life, with whom she had tramped the Greek hills, swam and fished in the Ionian Sea, and stolen honey from the big brown bees in the heather of Andelos. Nikos, with whom she had shared most of her joys and sorrows . . . whose loss to another girl had sent her on a voyage halfway round the world.

Domini had suggested that she take the trip, and Paul had been coaxed into putting at her disposal the trim little yacht that belonged to the chain of sea-going vessels run by the Stephanos Shipping Line.

Kara arranged the photograph on the table between the twin beds. When the yacht arrived back at Andelos, and the Captain informed Paul that she had disembarked at this island in the French Caribbean, there would be fireworks for Domini to deal with in her warm, calm, British way.

'My dear masterful man,' she would say to Paul, 'you must realize that Kara is twenty-one, a woman now with a mind of her own to make up. She wishes to be alone for a while. She needs to adjust to a future that will no longer hold Nikos. She will come to no harm—that dash of British blood from her mother dilutes her Greek impetuosity.'

Kara went to the dressing-table and studied her reflection in the mirror. She was as Greek as Paul to look at, but there were hints of her British blood in the small cleft in her chin, and in the shyness that sometimes made a veil of her thick dark lashes. Her figure was rather boyish, she thought, wrinkling her nose. She was as slim as a whip, but supple.

You swim like a seal, Nikos had often told her. You climb like a boy. In her innocence she had loved his compliments, but now she understood that if he had paid her compliments of a different kind, she might now be with him as his wife instead of being here . . . all alone.

Her fingers clenched the little crystal unicorn on her wrist-chain, a gift from Domini. 'A unicorn helped to bring me happiness,' she had told Kara softly. 'Happiness is very elusive, and sometimes we have to do battle with heartache before the unicorn works his magic for us.'

But at the moment Kara could not believe in a magic strong enough to mend a shattered dream. The broken pieces were hurting her heart even as she stood here, the brooding siesta calm broken only by the whisper of the fans and the cicadas in the trees outside. She went out on to her balcony and made her way down the winding iron stairs to the patio, where she curled herself beneath the awning of a swing-seat and rocked herself into semi-forgetfulness.

Guests at the Hotel Victoire were expected to take their meals in the rather bare dining-room, and as Kara sat down at a table and accepted a menu from the waiter, she ran her glance round the room. She saw a little sparse-haired man seated beside the other window, and a smile tugged at her lips. Was he the owner of the formidable name she had noticed in the register—Lucan Savidge, of Dragon Bay?

'Has *madame* decided?' The waiter hovered, his quick Creole eyes taking in her white linen suit with a pattern of tiny flowers on the collar.

'What is *lambi*?' she asked, intrigued.

'Ah, that is conch, *madame*, prepared the island way with spices and rice. You wish to order it?'

'Please. And—let me see—a cocktail of avocado and fresh shrimp to start with. I hope the conch meat doesn't taste too much like shrimp?'

'Ah, no.' The waiter was emphatic. '*Madame* will find that our Caribbean conch is delicious.'

It was mysteriously flavoured, she had to admit, and finishing her glass of *vin blanc*, she ordered coffee and sat gazing out of the window beside her table. Lights blinked along the waterfront, and upon the boats moored in the harbour, outlining their masts and casting goblin shapes on the water. The evening air that stole in through the open windows was spiced and tangy, scented by the tropical plants that seemed to breathe more freely now the sun had given place to a strolling moon.

It floated above the harbour, and spun a magical background for the palm and mango trees, whose tresses stirred now and again in a soft breeze.

The moonlight beckoned, and Kara was too restless to stay cooped up in the lounge of the hotel. She finished her coffee, collected a smile from the little Frenchman, and found Napoleon awaiting her behind his potted palm in the lobby. He jumped to his feet with alacrity when she appeared. 'I want you to show me Fort Fernand by moonlight, Nap,' she said.

They went out into the street together and strolled along trying to understand each other's French. A drawl with a yawn in it, that was the only way to describe the Creole accent, Kara thought, and pricked up her ears as she caught the word *fête*.

'A fair?' she said eagerly. 'I would love to see it, Nap.'

'So I was thinking,' the boy flashed her his impishly adult smile. 'Caribbean peoples make a lot of song and dance—is this not so where you come from, *mam'zelle*?'

'Yes, we like to sing and dance, Nap, but I suppose our gaiety has to have a reason. The birthday of a saint, or a wedding, or a birth. When my brother's little son was born, the people of our village danced all night, and there were firework displays, lantern-lit boats on the water, and lambs roasting whole with lemons in their jaws.'

She sighed nostalgically, remembering the happiness of that occasion, the joy in Paul's eyes.

10

'Your brother is important *seigneur?*' asked Nap.

'Yes,' she smiled. 'Important because we all love him, and respect him, and admire his great courage.'

'Like Seigneur Savidge,' said Nap. 'Here on the Isle de Luc he is ver' big man. Lots of people work for him. He has sugar estate at Dragon Bay, and big cocoa forest, and stables, but he—'

'Seigneur Savidge?' she exclaimed. 'Why, I saw his name in the hotel register.'

'That Massa Lucan, the *seigneur's* brother,' said the boy, and Kara saw the whites of his big black eyes as he looked at her. 'He a devil, *mam'zelle.* He ride all over the island on a big horse, and a big hound run alongside. He done things people whisper about.'

Nap's voice sank down into a whisper that made the remark curiously effective. Lucan Savidge . . . as savage as his name implied.

Then Kara forgot about him as she and Napoleon arrived at the fair, which was encamped on a *savane* above the harbour, aglow with lights, gay with laughter and noise. They passed a small compound, ringed by people watching a mongoose fight a snake. Kara shuddered and pulled Nap towards the

11

blare of music where a roundabout swung and swayed. They went on when it stopped, and for some odd reason Kara chose a fiery dragon for her mount and laughed breathlessly as the great creature hurtled and undulated to the rhythm of the music.

'You like?' yelled Nap, clinging to the neck of a sea-horse.

'I like.' Her eyes were bright in the streaming lights, and her heart felt lighter than it had for some time. She had been right to choose this place! She had known from the moment the yacht put into Fort Fernand that there was something *beckoning* about this Caribbean isle.

Faster and faster hurled the dragon, higher and more ecstatic rang the screams of honey and sable girls, and with a sudden stab of wonderment Kara recognized the music to which she and her dragon raced—*Holiday of a Faun.*

Dry-throated after the thrill of the roundabout, she and Nap bought bottles of Coke and strolled along sucking it from straws. Couples were dancing in another compound, while lithe young men pounded the tom-toms gripped between their knees. Lantern light shone on bare brown torsos, the beat of the drums was pagan and compulsive. Flame flared on the limbo poles as youths and girls snaked beneath them and leapt with agility, white teeth flashing, into the rhythm of the Creole dancing.

A little further on, where the *savane* rolled down to meet the water, the tent of the 'sibyl' was pitched and girls were sliding in and out of the tent flaps with infectious giggles.

'You going to have your fortune told by Mamma Mae?' Nap gave Kara a saucy look.

'It's all nonsense.' Kara laughed, but her eyes were sombre as she remembered the gipsy who had said that one day she would travel across water with a tall, dark man. Nikos had travelled alone across the water, and when he returned to the Greek isle of Andelos, he would bring his golden bride with him. A sigh stole from Kara's lips, and she heard small waves beat at the harbour wall below like restless hands.

'You scared?' Nap taunted.

'Of course not.' Kara took a step away from the tent. 'Come on, it's time we returned to the hotel——' Even as she spoke, the tent flap moved, but this time a woman appeared, wearing a turban tied in the Creole way with horns. She was gaunt, with a penetrating gaze in a mask of wrinkles.

'Come inside, *doudou*.' A flick of those

13

dark eyes took in Kara's smart linen suit. 'Let Mamma Mae read your palm for you.'

'No—I don't believe in such nonsense,' Kara said defiantly. 'I have heard before about the tall stranger I am to meet.'

Mamma Mae stared at Kara, then shot a glance at Nap, while the thudding of tom-toms beat in time to the girl's heart. 'You stay at Hotel Victoire, eh?' The sibyl gave a laugh that shook the big rings in her ears. 'You 'bout ready to meet this man, honey—onless you leave Isle de Luc. He got fire in his hair—plenty fire.'

With a swish the tent flaps closed together, and Kara tilted her chin in scorn. 'Well, it's a change from being dark and handsome,' she said. 'Come, Nap!' The boy fell into step beside her as she hastened away from the fair. They didn't speak on the way back to the hotel, and then in the lobby Nap gave Kara a curious look.

'You leaving Isle de Luc, *mam'zelle?*' he asked.

'Of course not.' She turned at the foot of the stairs to look at him in surprise, the key to her room in her hand. 'Will there be bath water tonight, Nap? Nice warm bath water?'

He nodded. She smiled and told him to run off to bed.

14

'Goodnight, *mam'zelle*.' He gazed at her with his big dark eyes, the edges of his jeans halfway up his shanks, his check shirt slipping half off his thin young shoulders.

'*Kale nichta*, Napoleon.' She made her way upstairs to her room on the second floor, which had a gilt 16 nailed to the door. She felt tired but restless, and knew that only a warm bath would make it possible for her to sleep. She reached the second floor and took note of each number on the bedroom doors as she passed them. The corridor was very quiet and she had a feeling most of the rooms were unoccupied. The bathroom was situated at the end of the corridor, and she heard plainly the sound of the shower as she unlocked her door and switched on the light of her room.

She hoped the occupant of the shower would not be long, and was in her bathrobe when a door slammed along the corridor. It was a rather arrogant slam, as though the person involved did not trouble much about disturbing the dreams of other people. Kara stood holding her sponge-bag and bath-towel, then she opened her own door and listened for the sound of the shower. All was still and quiet, and switching out her light she left the moon in occupancy of her room and went along to take a bath.

15

The user of the shower had splashed energetically and left large wet footprints all over the dark tiling of the floor. A man, Kara thought, shaking her head as she turned the tap of the old-fashioned tub and sprinkled pine-scented crystals into the steaming water. She breathed deeply of the pine, and was wafted in imagination to the woods of Andelos, where pine trees grew in abundance, tall and aromatic.

Tears filled her eyes and she blinked them away impatiently. Even if she had wanted to leave the Isle de Luc, her brother's yacht had left and she was committed to the impulse which had brought her ashore. She must stay tonight, at any rate, and a pine-scented soak would induce the good night's rest she needed.

Almost an hour later, pink and sleepy, she yawned her way out of the bathroom and made for Number 16. Ah, there it was. She had not locked her door and upon slipping inside she tossed off her bathrobe without bothering to switch on the light. The moon cast enough of a glow for her to feel her way into the nearest of the single beds. Tiredness clung to her senses like cobwebs, and with a little sigh of relief she settled down to sleep, slim and lost beneath the pavilion of tropical netting.

A travelling clock ticked on the table between the two beds, and there wafted in from the balcony of the room the smoke of a cheroot, but Kara did not smell it. And when in a while a tall figure loomed against the moonlight, she wasn't aware. She slept on—a small figure lost beneath cloudy netting—unseen by the man who tossed off his pyjama jacket and slid beneath the netting of the other twin bed.

CHAPTER TWO

KARA awoke suddenly. Fingers had rapped the door and now it opened and a voice said: 'Your morning coffee, *m'sieur*.'

The figure of a waiter appeared outside her netting, then he was between the beds and Kara drew aside the netting to let him see that she was not a *m'sieur*. She was about to reach for the cup of coffee, when to her utter consternation the netting of the other bed parted and a muscular male arm reached out for the cup and saucer. A tousled head and a broad pair of shoulders appeared at the same time, and Kara felt a shock to her marrowbone as she met the eyes of the man in the bed.

His eyes were a diamond-hard grey with green fires at their depths. They held her motionless as they flicked her hair, her mouth, the open collar of her pyjamas, and came back again to make captives of her immense Greek eyes. 'Another cup of coffee for the young lady,' he said calmly to the waiter.

'Of course, *m'sieur*.' A knowing smile flitted across the waiter's face. The door closed behind him, and Kara was alone with

18

the lordly stranger whose dark red hair curled close to his scalp, and who looked as though he had never been embarrassed in his life.

'How unexpected.' He spoke in French, though she had the feeling he was not a Frenchman. 'A guest for breakfast.'

Kara sat gaping at him as though he were speaking Hottentot, and then her voice came back with a rush. 'This is my room,' she gasped. 'What do you think you are doing in it?'

'I am sorry to contradict a lady,' he looked sorry about nothing, and his smile was dangerous, 'but this happens to be *my* room. Take a look around you.'

She did so and alarm flooded her. There was a man's white shirt thrown carelessly over the back of a chair, brushes and belongings on the dressing table that were undoubtedly masculine, and *no* happy family photograph on the bed-table. A blush of intense confusion ran from Kara's throat to her temples.

'I'm so sorry—' She started to scramble out of the bed she had no right in, and in a voice like the flick of a whip he ordered her to stay where she was. His grey-green eyes were on her feet, poised like startled birds just above the floor.

19

'What absurdly small feet,' he said, and then his eyes were raking her lingering blush. 'You are not an *amoureuse*, I take it?'

'Are you disappointed?' she flashed. 'This is a genuine mistake, *m'sieur*. I—I must have mistaken the number of your door for mine.'

'My number is nineteen. What is yours?'

'Sixteen.' Her eyes were like those of a trapped forest creature as she watched him swing out of bed and stride in bare feet and torso to the door. He swung it open and took a look. Then he laughed. It was deep-throated, devilish, as though he enjoyed a situation that put other people at his mercy.

'The number 9 must have been loose,' he drawled. 'It has dropped down and it looks like a 6—all the same, young lady, you are not leaving my room just yet.'

'W-what do you mean?' She scrambled instinctively behind the bedclothes as the door snapped shut and he stood with his back to it, tall, with wide ranging shoulders and a deep chest. His waist and hips were lean in comparison ... there was a rampant maleness about him, a sun- and wind-browned look of a man who spent most of his life in the open air.

'If you were a gentleman,' Kara could feel her toes curling beneath the bedcovers, 'you would let me return to my room this

20

instant—'

'Don't you think I look a gentleman?' His left eyebrow quirked wickedly above mocking green eyes, and as Kara looked at him a pulse beat quickly under the clear honey skin of her throat.

'You look as though you could be a devil,' she gasped, 'but a waiter is on his way with another cup of coffee—and I have a good pair of lungs for screaming.'

'How Victorian and amusing, coming from a girl who has just spent the night in a stranger's bedroom,' he mocked. 'I don't think the waiter would be very impressed by your screams—being a Frenchman he would assume that it was a little late for you to be rescued. *Que c'est risqué*, little one, to get involved with Lucan Savidge. The people of the Isle de Luc will tell you that he asks mercy of no one, and gives none in return.'

'You are Lucan Savidge?' she exclaimed.

'At your service.' He gave her a mock bow, and despite the fact that he was wearing only black silk pyjamas there was about him the assured, plantocratic look of a man who was used to giving orders, who liked spirited horses to ride, and red wine in crystal. Kara scanned the strong, tanned bone structure of his features, and she could well believe that he made his own rules and lived by them.

'I can see that you have heard of me, though you are a newcomer to the Isle de Luc.' As he spoke, he drew away from the door and shrugged into a dressing-gown and sought his slippers. He seemed to take it for granted that having ordered her to stay where she was, she would do so and not make a dart for the door. The urge to escape was strong in her, but instinct warned her that she dealt with a man as quick and tempered as a jungle cat. He would leap after her and take hold of her with his large brown hands . . . a thought that made her go small in the bed that was only a yard or so from his bed. He sat down on the side of it and appraised her.

'I can't quite place your nationality,' he said, 'but you put me in mind of a faun. Is it your ears, or your eyes?'

'My name is Kara Stephanos,' she said with dignity. 'I am taking a holiday in the Caribbean, and my homeland is Greece.'

'Ah,' his eyebrows slanted together, darker than the foxfire of his hair, 'so you are Grecian. Is there not a Greek word for the fateful chance that throws two people together?'

She gazed at him with wide and wondering eyes. 'The word is *moira*,' she said, and was both relieved and confused to hear a tap on the door, followed by a discreet cough and the entrance of the waiter. He carried a laden tray.

'I took the liberty, *m'sieur*, of bringing breakfast—for two.'

There was a pot of coffee on the tray, hot *croissants*, butter and fruit. There were two cups, two plates, and an unconcealed smile in the waiter's eyes as they flicked from Lucan Savidge to Kara. Her cheeks burned. Nap had said last night that the man with the savage name was a man people whispered about.

* * *

'The sun is on the balcony, so we will eat our breakfast there.' Lucan Savidge gestured at the bathrobe Kara had tossed off last night, so sleepy from the fun of the fair, and her bath, that she had wandered into a stranger's bedroom and spent the night there.

Her breath caught in her throat, for as she followed the tall stranger on to his balcony the sun fired his hair and she remembered the sibyl's warning. She had spoken of an encounter with a man with fire in his hair; she had advised Kara to leave Fort Fernand before morning.

Kara had not heeded her warning; now

23

morning had come and she had encountered Lucan Savidge with a vengeance.

He pulled out a wicker chair from the matching table, and Kara slipped into it. The sun was in the crests of the patio palm trees, and little tongues of fire peeped from the hibiscus bells. The sky was a clear, reassuring blue, and Kara felt much safer out here under the sky with this intimidating man.

She poured their coffee and watched him break a *croissant* and spread it with butter. 'It is curious that we should be sitting here like this.' A smile turned to a glint in his eyes. 'I would be very suspicious if you were not so— but then *coquettes* have been known to be innocent-looking.'

'I shall have my cup of coffee and then go,' she said coldly. 'No doubt you are a good catch, Monsieur Savidge, but a *coquette* would have to be innocent if she thought *you* could be compromised.'

'You don't like me at all, do you?' He smiled and added brown island sugar to his coffee. 'You are thinking that if I were gallant I would not have allowed the waiter to assume the obvious. My dear girl, I could hardly smuggle you back to your room as though the fellow had not seen you at all—looking all big-eyed and fluffy in the bed next to mine.'

Kara took several quick sips of her coffee. 'You could have explained that you slammed your door last night and made the number 9 fall down to form a 6, and that I mistook your room for mine.'

'Why did you stay silent when you could have given the same explanation?' he inquired.

'I—I was lost for words,' she said helplessly. 'Try being a girl—though I can see that would be hard—who wakes up in a strange hotel to find she has slept all night beside a stranger.'

His answering laughter relished the situation.

'I shall leave the Isle de Luc today,' she said.

He stopped laughing and his fingers paused on the mandarin he was peeling. 'Running away?' he taunted.

She flicked crumbs off the table and did not answer.

'Is that why you are here on the Isle de Luc?' His glance seemed to touch her skin like the flick of a whip. 'Are you already in the process of running away from someone?'

'It's none of your business, Mr. Savidge.' She bore his scrutiny as long as she could, then flushed and looked away from him. The sun was firing the sea, but she felt too disturbed to appreciate the view from Lucan Savidge's balcony. Her love for Nikos, his love for someone else, was something she could not talk about to this man who looked as though he had never loved anyone.

'Don't worry, little martyr eyes,' he mocked, 'your girlish romance is of no interest to me. But what of your family? Don't they mind that you are alone in the Caribbean, where men of my stamp are likely to be met with?'

'Sugar kings, *m'sieur*? I thought they were part of another century, another time. I had no idea they still ruled in Great Houses amidst their canefields and cocoa groves.'

His mouth pulled to one side in a smile that left his eyes a cool grey-green. 'The Savidges of Dragon Bay are part of the history of this island,' he said. 'Our roots go deep into the soil with the cane and the cocoa. We came from Ireland as rebels, and we stayed to found a dynasty.'

'On slave owning?' she said scornfully.

'The Caribs were our workers and we never made slaves of them.' Now he was looking arrogant—cool, hard and arrogant, his wicker chair tipped back against the ironwork of the balcony. 'I asked you a question about

26

your family. Do they let a child like you roam where she pleases?'

'In the first place I am not a child, Mr. Savidge. In the second place my parents are dead.' She wiped the juice of a paw-paw from her lips. 'Nap, the young boy who works here, told me about your brother—'

'About him being crippled,' the deep voice bit out the words, 'and that I was blamed for his accident?'

'You were blamed?' Kara's dark eyes seemed to devour the fine contours of her face.

'Yes.' Lucan Savidge surged to his feet and towered over the table, his hair a brand in the sunlight, his eyes fiercely alight, the hard bones jutting beneath the sun-browned skin of his face.

'Yes,' he said again, and he stared past Kara to where the sky met the sea far out. 'We used to be inseparable, Pryde and I. We rode our horses like a pair of demons, we did everything together, trying I suppose to outdo one another in daring and skill. We thought of ourselves as out of the age of heroes and giants because we were the Savidge twins. We shared a common heritage, a worship of our history and our home.'

He began to pace back and forth, and Kara

27

sat watching him from her seat at the table, her chin propped on her hand.

'It wasn't until I was seventeen,' he said, 'that I fully realized that Pryde was the heir to all I loved because he was the elder by an hour. Our Negro *Da* was annoyed with me for the usual reason that I was never as tidy as my brother. "Good t'ing you born last," she said. "Pryde is more fittin' to be master at Dragon Bay".'

'It hit me, slashed at me like a whip. Close as I was to Pryde, I was brought to my knees that day by the painful realization that we did not share everything. We were home from our school for the holidays and running wild as usual, and I agreed when Pryde challenged me to a climb up the cliffs that rise sheer from the side of Dragon Bay to the crest on which the Great House stands. We always said that one day we would attempt the climb. It was a challenge, and I felt utterly reckless of the consequences—if one of us fell.'

Kara heard the harsh sigh that left the hard lips of this man she had met so strangely. She couldn't take her eyes from him . . . her heart felt as though it were beating in her throat, and quite unaware her hand was holding her throat.

'God's heaven, if only a point in time could

28

be erased, never to have been.' Lucan Savidge leaned his arms on the balcony rail and his brooding profile was turned to Kara, hard-boned, with a small crescent of a scar standing out against the tanned skin. 'Those with Irish blood in their veins have premonitions of trouble, and I had one as Pryde and I began to climb that cliff. Being twins we shared some of our emotions, and Pryde gave a laugh as he swung himself upwards. "You look chickeny," he said. "Want to cry off—little brother?"'

'It was always "little brother" when Pryde was feeling cocky about that hour's difference in our ages, and I was still choked up from what *Da* had thrown in my face. "I'll be first in this if it kills one of us," I threw back at him. I climbed as though I had a whip across my shoulders, and we were three-quarters of the way up, and I had a short lead on Pryde, when—when Pryde had his fall!'

Lucan Savidge swung round to face Kara, and only once before in her life had she seen that expression of naked regret on a person's face. 'Pryde fell to the rocks and broke his back,' he said harshly.

'*Oh no!*' Kara masked her eyes with her hand, for something was in them, a blaze of something she had to hide from this man who

29

told her these things because—like passengers on a ship or a plane—they would not meet again when they parted.

'You could never have seen a wild young stag crashing into a net in wildest pain.' The Irish imagery made the scene unbearably vivid for Kara. 'Your heart can ache for the strong with much more intensity than for the weak.'

'Yes, I know.' She spoke huskily, and remembered the pain of seeing her brother Paul lying helpless in a hospital bed, robbed of his strength, and having that strength put back by the love and the will that blazed in Domini.

'Your brother did not die,' she said.

'No.' Stamped on the lean brown face was an expression of irony and pain. 'Fate is the great *farceur*. It can take a whole man and turn him into half a man within the same time that it takes you or me to take a bite out of an apple. Pryde has the use of his upper body; from the waist down he is helpless.'

'Dante's "dark wood midway in the journey of our life",' Kara murmured. 'Your story is a terrible one, Mr. Savidge.'

'And I am a terrible person, eh?'

She looked at him gravely, but could not put into words what she thought. He was pacing the sun-shot balcony, vital and restless as a caged creature—more caged than the brother in his wheelchair, for his was the innocence, this man's the guilt. It would always be the guilt because he had gone on with the climb; because he had said he would win if it killed one of them.

Jealous as Lucan! He was aptly named.

She jumped to her feet. 'I—I must go, *m'sieur*.' She addressed him that way because she had glimpsed the Gallic in him, wedded to the Gaelic. 'To say it is a shame about your brother would be inadequate, but don't— please don't be too bitter.'

She was making for the stairs that led down to the patio, and then up again to her room, when in a stride he barred her way. 'You can't just go,' he said. 'We must meet again. To-night. We'll dine together—not here at the hotel but somewhere else.'

'I don't think it would be wise for us to meet again—' her dark eyes lifted to his face with its sun-darkened features, a small etching of lines beside the crystal-green eyes, the scar on his cheekbone adding to his diablerie.

'I think we must.' His fingers shackled her wrist, and she knew it to be an inescapable grip though his touch was only a promise of steel against her wristbone. 'Are you afraid of

31

me, Kara—or of yourself?'

'W-what nonsense!' The jerk of her heart was in her voice. 'Please let me go, Mr. Savidge. You have had your fun in keeping me here, and I have listened to you and been sympathetic—'

'Sympathy?' he laughed, a flash of scorn in his eyes. 'Do you think I care two hoots about that? I told you about Pryde's fall because I wanted you to know exactly the kind of man I am—because I want no secrets between us. We will meet again this evening.'

'No—' she tried to wrench away from him, and in an instant, with the strength of the uncaring, he caught her to him and she felt as though her bones would give way.

'This evening,' he repeated. 'Don't run away, Kara, because if you do, you will always wonder what I might have asked of you.'

'Why should I wonder, or care?' Her voice shook with angry fear, and close to him she was aware of a strength and resolution she had never felt in Nikos. 'Do you think I owe you something because of last night?'

'Perhaps we owe last night to forces we shouldn't oppose.' A smile pulled his mouth to one side. 'Are you worried about the wagging tongues of Fort Fernand? Running away

32

won't set them at rest.'

'It won't set them at rest if I stay,' she rejoined.

'Do you care what other people say about you?' He tilted back her head with his hand, and his gaze travelled from her eyes to her lips. 'People have been saying things about me for years. Do you know how I got the scar on my cheek? My own mother lashed me when I ran to the Great House to give the alarm about Pryde. She was in the hall, still in her riding clothes, and she lashed me across the face and said that the Savidge Dragon always took care of his own.'

He laughed, deeply, carelessly, then he let go of Kara and made for the door that led into his room. 'Go on, little girl, run away,' he threw over his shoulder.

She ran down the patio steps and up the other side, and she didn't look back. Safe in her room, with *her* clothes scattered about, and that reassuring family group on the bed-table, she breathed with shaky relief. She would leave the Isle de Luc today, before she got involved any further with Lucan Savidge.

She was throwing her belongings into the suitcase she had unpacked yesterday, when there was a tap on her door. *'Entrez!'* she called out.

33

Nap came into the room, carrying a sealed envelope with her name scrawled across the front of it. 'You want guide for the day, *mam'zelle?*' He handed her the envelope and gazed hopefully at her.

'No,' her fingers clenched the envelope. 'No, I don't think so, Nap.'

'Okay. I around if you change yo' mind.'

Directly the door closed behind Nap, Kara tore open the envelope and withdrew the folded note inside. The writing on it was dark and decisive. 'Let me at least give you a farewell dinner,' Lucan Savidge had written. 'To say good-bye, as the French say, is to die a little.'

There ran through Kara a swift urge to tear the note in shreds, to save herself from another meeting with the unsettling stranger whose face was etched with disturbing clarity in her mind's eye. Her fingers crushed his note. Why should she care if a stranger went to the devil because of something that had happened when she was still a schoolgirl, running wild with Nikki on the island of Andelos? She had a hurt of her own to get over. . . .

She sank down on the side of the nearest bed and stared at the floor. It flooded over her in cold little waves that Nikos was far away, and now the husband of a girl called Cicely.

Nikki, with his long, lively face that was so good-looking when he laughed.

She tried to bring his face into focus, but the brown eyes went diamond-hard and green; the boyish features hardened and grew bolder, beneath a crest of foxfire hair.

Lucan Savidge . . . a man whom people spoke about in whispers, who carried on his cheekbone the mark of his mother's whip.

*   *   *

There is only a little dusk in the tropics. The sun shatters in a web of colours, and then night falls and the stars come out, a retinue for the moon this second night of Kara's visit to the Isle de Luc.

The small open carriage drew up at the entrance of the Painted Lantern, and white teeth flashed against an ebony face as the driver accepted his fare from Kara's escort. Then the whip lightly cracked and the horse-drawn carriage moved off.

'The last time I drove in one of those was in Athens.' Kara bit her lip, for Nikos had been with her instead of a tall, wide-shouldered man in cream drill worn with a brown silk shirt and tie. She felt his fingers under her elbow as they entered the restaurant, and was

35

very aware of how erect and lithe he was.

'I promised you an unusual evening,' he said, and her eyes widened as she gazed around the softly lit room, with teakwood tables in alcoves, bird-painted screens, and pergolas entwined in frangipani. Coming towards them was a Mandarin figure in a long silk gown, long-nailed hands clasped together, his smile oblique as he bowed them to a secluded table.

'It is a great pleasure to see you again in my humble restaurant, Mr. Savidge,' he said.

'It is my pleasure, Mr. Yen, to be a visitor again in your house of soft lights and excellent food. I hope you have duck meat with lotus seeds on your menu tonight?'

'Always we have what your heart most desires.' The Mandarin figure bowed again, and his eyes were dark as lacquer as he smiled and clapped his hands for a waiter. Hands that might have been painted by a brush-stroke artist.

Kara let out her breath very slowly as the silk-robed Mr. Yen was lost behind a beaded curtain. 'Did I dream him?' she murmured, a small, shy smile in her eyes. Am I dreaming? she wondered. Did I really agree to dine with a man who looks fierce even by oriental lantern light?

As if reading her thoughts, he gazed deliberately across at her and took in her simple dress tied at the waist with cherry ribbons—a little-girl dress, which she had donned deliberately.

'Have you ever had Chinese food?' he asked.

She shook her head.

'Then it will be a new experience for you.' And something in his voice, his eyes, seemed to add that experiences shared with him would all be new to her. Her heart beat as rapidly as a cicada wing, and she glanced away from the lean, audacious face with its mark of Cain.

'A menu, sir, and one for *madame*.' A Chinese waiter was at the table, and Kara opened her menu and gazed in perplexity at the Chinese script.

'Will you put yourself in my hands?' asked Lucan Savidge, and again she was aware of some deeper shade of meaning in his deep voice.

'Yes, you choose my dinner for me.' Her smile pulled at the nerves of her lips. 'Only don't order anything too exotic.'

'Are you scared to take a chance?' he mocked. 'A girl from the land of pagan gods and nymphs.'

'That was long ago, Mr. Savidge. Now our gods are domesticated and our nymphs very cautious,' she said demurely.

'How disappointing.' There were green devils in his eyes as he looked across at her, then he turned to the waiter and Kara listened as he ordered—she was sure—the most exotic edibles on the menu.

'Do you want to try bamboo *k'uai tzu*?' he asked solemnly.

'Whatever does that taste like?' As she looked at him, wrinkling a dubious nose, he laughed. She glanced at the waiter and saw a smile in his oblique eyes.

'*K'uai tzu* are chopsticks, *madame*.' A slight inclination of his head made her look in the direction of a nearby table, where a couple were eating with dexterous movements of their chopsticks.

'Bring two pairs with the *chow fan*,' ordered Lucan Savidge. 'And rice wine right away, to settle madame's nerves for the ordeal in store for her.'

'What a terrible person you are!' Kara said, when the waiter had left them alone. 'I think you enjoy making a fool of women.'

'You look like a small girl,' he said carelessly. 'How did the knight of your girlish dreams treat you, as a rose, waiting in your bower of thorns to be plucked? Is that why you ran away from him, because he hesitated a little too long?'

'I don't intend to share with you what is private to me,' she said tensely, and her nostrils flared with anger and the fragrance of the witch-white frangipani.

'We can't pretend to be strangers, Kara.' He smiled devilishly. 'Last night we shared the same room, remember. What would your Greek sweetheart have to say to that?'

'Very little, Mr. Savidge.' Her lips were tense around the words. 'Nikos happens to be married to someone else, if you must know. He met her in America, and she possesses all that I could never hope to compete with—golden hair, a perfect figure, and a lovely face.'

'So if you had golden hair you would now be wearing a golden ring?' Lucan Savidge looked quizzical. 'How long have you known this boy?'

'All my life.'

'And you think your heart is broken, eh?'

'I think you are the most cynical man I have ever met,' she flashed. 'I don't think you have a heart to break.'

He quirked an eyebrow, and then said lazily: 'Here comes the waiter with our wine.

It is called *Shau-shing*, and is said to warm the coldest heart—not mine, of course.' His teeth flashed white against his tanned face. 'I tick over on a different system from other people.'

The warm amber wine was poured into little porcelain wine cups, and Kara was shown how to raise the cup lightly in her hands and to drink every drop with a backward tilt of her head. The oriental wine caressed her throat and then ran like a gentle fire through her veins. A pleasant sensation that soothed away her tenseness.

Their *chow-fan* was a delectable mixture of spiced egg and rice, and Kara found that if she picked up small pieces with her chopsticks and held the bowl near her chin, some of the *chow-fan* found its way into her mouth.

'You had better use a spoon,' said her companion drily.

'No.' She shook her head. 'I am just beginning to get the knack. Mmmm, this is tasty.'

Afterwards they had duck with lotus seeds, tiny mushrooms, and other vegetables she could not name, and then a dessert into which pieces of ginger had been inserted. It wasn't until their hands had been refreshed by hot towels, and Chinese tea brought to the table, that Kara realized how the meal had relaxed

40

her. She breathed the jasmine in her bowl of tea, and listened as Lucan Savidge talked of his home at Dragon Bay.

It stood on a crest above the plantations of sugar and cocoa, and a drive bordered by Royal Palms led to a columned portico and a great front door of teakwood, enduring as the stone of which the house was built. It was three-winged, with covered flagstone walks joining the wings to the grand patio.

'It might be a Babylonian palace from your description of it,' Kara smiled.

'It stands out against the blue sky like a feudal stronghold—it even has a ghost.' His smile was a sideways pull of his bold, hard lips. 'A lady dressed in gold, who steps out of a painted window above the stairs. She died tragically in a fire at the old sugar mill, where she was said to meet her lover.'

'How fascinating.' Kara's gaze fell away from his and she sipped at her jasmine tea, aware of the quickening of her pulses, of the magnetism this man could exert when he was in the mood. 'You must love your home very much,' she murmured.

'Can a man without a heart love anything?'

She glanced up, into eyes that were as cool and still as sea-water that holds unimaginable depths and danger. 'It's a mistake to think

that we know anyone,' she said, 'and a pre-
sumption to pass judgment on an ac-
quaintance of only a few hours. You must
forgive my Greek impetuosity, Mr. Savidge.'

'Are you often impetuous?' He signalled
their waiter as he spoke, and she assumed that
he was about to settle the bill and announce
that their farewell dinner was over.

'I sometimes do things that I don't stop to
think about,' she admitted. 'It is in the Stephanos blood—my father married my mother
after knowing her only ten days. She was
English, but I am mostly Greek.'

Lucan Savidge ran his green eyes over
Kara's long dark hair, pale gold skin, and tiny
rings in the lobes of her ears. 'When the
waiter brings our liqueur,' he said, 'he will
also bring the fortune cards. The Chinese are
great believers in omens and portents—are
the Greeks?'

'But of course.' She gave a slightly nervous
laugh, for at the fair last night a dark sibyl
had forecast a strange meeting that had come
about. A meeting with a man whose hair in
the lantern light held glints of fire; whose
rebel ancestors had clawed what they had out
of the very earth and set their nest high, like
eagles.

Their Chinese waiter brought the fortune

42

cards to the table, and there was a rattle of a bead curtain as Mr. Yen reappeared, solemn as a Mandarin. He poured their liqueur from a lovely old stone bottle and handed one cup to Kara and the other to her companion. They drank in unison, and then they each took a card from the pack and placed it on the table for Mr. Yen to interpret.

It was an intriguing game and nothing more, Kara told herself, but all the same her heart beat fast and her eyes dwelt wonderingly on the oriental figure in the wide-sleeved gown. 'I see a feast of lanterns in the house of the dragon,' he murmured. 'Tell me, young lady, do you expect soon to attend a wedding?'

'A—wedding?' Her fingers clenched around her wine cup. 'It has already taken place, Mr. Yen. I could not attend because it took place a long way from where I live.'

Mr. Yen tapped her fortune card with a long index nail, and then he nodded. 'Yes, some of the lanterns are dark, so someone has wept.' With a swift movement he turned Kara's card face down and gave his attention to that of Lucan Savidge, who sat regarding the procedure with a sardonic expression in his eyes.

'Am I to be wedded, or wept over?' he

murmured, with his sideways pull of a smile. 'Both would be unique procedures.'

'I fear that you have chosen the gambler's card, Mr. Savidge. You must choose another—'

'No.' Lucan Savidge shook his head and gave a laugh that held a note of savagery. 'Fate's a tiger, Mr. Yen, and something tells me tonight not to look it in the teeth.'

'As you wish.' Mr. Yen bowed and swept the cards all together. 'I hope the humble service and food of the Painted Lantern did not disappoint either of you?'

'The meal was out of this world, Mr. Yen, and the service beyond reproach.'

'It was delicious,' said Kara with a shy smile. 'I shall take away a fascinating memory when I leave the Isle de Luc.'

A few minutes later she and Lucan Savidge left behind them the soft lights of the Painted Lantern, and the scent of frangipani, a flower out of pagan temples.

They walked along the waterfront, where the rigging of a sloop was ablaze with fairy lights and noisy with song and laughter. A party was in progress and Kara could see couples dancing together on the deck, some cheek to cheek, others apart in the modern manner, swinging their hips to the Caribbean

44

rhythm.

'Well,' said Lucan Savidge, 'what do you think of the Caribbean?'

'It is colourful, interesting—and unexpected.' The music died away behind them, and he gave her a hand down some shadowy steps to the beach. The sands crunched beneath their shoes, and the moonlight hung in the crests of the palm trees, slender and always slightly bowed before the wind gods.

'But all the same you intend to leave.' He bent and picked up a conch-shell and she heard his fingers scraping at the sand on it. 'Will our unexpected encounter be among the memories you spoke of taking away with you?'

'Yes,' she said honestly. 'How could I forget this morning, or this evening at the Painted Lantern? Or a man with unhappy memories?'

'The deeper the scar, the harder grows the skin,' he mocked. He handed her the empty conch-shell and told her to hold it to her ear. 'What do you hear?' he asked.

'The sea in huge breakers, pounding,' she said after a moment.

'Like the sea beyond Dragon Bay,' he murmured.

'Why do you stay at the Hotel Victoire

when your home is at Dragon Bay?' she asked curiously.

'I have been on a trip, and I go home next week by Carib raft.' He slanted her a smile, his face lean and rakish in the moonlight, his eyes a haunting green. 'Sounds primitive to you, perhaps, but the journey to our bay is always made in the old way. It is part of the Savidge tradition; a need in the blood to cling to the colourful and to repudiate the machine age.'

'I can understand,' she said. 'Back home in Greece I love all the old ways. The goat-boy piping in the hills. The olive harvest and the engagements that always seem to follow. Swimming at night in the purple-dark water and grabbing handfuls of reflected stars.'

'The Caribbean at night is like champagne to swim in.' He stood tall beside Kara, gazing out across the water, and her glance was free to roam the moon-etched line of his profile. Boldly defined, with a rebel's mouth that never smiled without irony. His hair a helmet of bronze, his strong throat merging into a deep chest against which long ago he would have carried a bull-hide shield. . . .

Odd thoughts, which caused her to be suddenly aware of their isolation on this beach. They had wandered a long way from the lights of the town, and there are few things more intimate than a honey moon above water, and a girl alone with a man who slightly un-nerves her.

'We should start walking back,' she suggested. 'It's late, and I intend to leave early tomorrow—'

'Don't leave.' He swung to face her, and he wasn't smiling or coaxing, or looking anything but rather harsh. 'Don't run away from the Isle de Luc because of other people and what they may think.'

'It isn't that,' she protested.

'Is it me?' He came a step closer, and Kara had to fight not to retreat from his tall, arrogant figure. 'Or is it that you've cocooned yourself from more hurt, and I look the sort who hurts?'

'Nikos did not mean to hurt me,' she defended him quickly. 'It was just that his heart wanted someone else—hearts are like that, they open a little way to some, and all the way to others.'

'And with your heart left empty, you are now roaming through the Caribbean enjoying a little martyrdom?' he said sarcastically. 'Empty rooms invite cobwebs and echoes, Kara, and you strike me as too vibrant and alive to want an unfulfilled emptiness inside you.'

She shivered, and saw the loneliness of the sea, still and sobbing a little under the distant caress of the moon. Nikki, cried her heart, why did you take me half-way into your heart and then reject me?

'Wherever you go,' said Lucan Savidge, 'the memories will follow. *I know.*'

She looked at him and wondered what it was he wanted of her, a stranger without the prettiness that might attract a casual affair. A girl on the run from all those who knew how she had worshipped a tall boy with black hair and a gay, lopsided smile.

She gazed with inquiring eyes at this man whose memories were more ruthless than her own. She knew about the myths that could surround a strong and picturesque personality; how they could grow from threads into cords that strangled the real truth. What was the real truth? Was this man so savage . . . or did he guard a heart as broken as his brother's body?

'Next week I go home to Dragon Bay,' he said. 'Why not stay until then, Kara, and let me show you around Fort Fernand?'

In the breeze along the shore, a lovelock danced on her forehead. Her throat tightened, for something in his voice had got to her and shaken her resolve to leave the Isle de Luc.

'Perhaps,' she said. 'I don't suppose I shall find anything more or less on any other island. The sun will shine as bright, the palms will bow to the same wind-gods, and the sea will be as good to bathe in.'

'Did you know,' said Lucan Savidge, as they turned in unison to walk back towards the town, 'that all islands are supposed to be flung up by wrathful sea-gods?'

She smiled and listened to the sea-talk within the conch-shell he had given her. Angry, a roar in it, like the waters of Dragon Bay. She was still carrying the shell when they paused outside her room at the Hotel Victoire. 'The number 9 has been nailed back into position on your door,' she said.

'So I noticed.' His smile made creases at either side of his mouth, there was a winged devilry to his brows, a wickedly amused gleam in his eyes.

Kara unlocked her door and withdrew inside. 'Thank you for taking me to the Painted Lantern,' she spoke rather breathlessly. 'It was an unusual experience.'

'Because of the food, the fortune, or the company?' He leant forward and flicked his eyes over her face. 'Well, Kara?'

49

Her fingers tightened on the handle of her door and she wanted to ask him why he wanted her company. Was he just amusing himself with an unsophisticated girl, or did he need her friendship? If only she could be sure, but Lucan Savidge had a face that was not easy to read. A lean, hard face, with a whip scar on the right cheekbone, and eyes that changed in different lights from green to the colour of stone.

'You think too much, do you know that?' He laughed, and it seemed to her that he laughed carelessly, as though it didn't really matter to him whether she stayed tomorrow or left.

'You are a man who sets one thinking,' she rejoined. 'I have the feeling that you treat everyone as a game—what game, Mr. Savidge, are you playing with me?'

'The game of guide and tourist, Miss Stephanos,' he replied. 'Don't you fancy to stay, after all? Are you afraid of me—of getting involved with a man instead of a boy?'

'Oh—' Colour came into her cheeks. 'You really are a devil!'

'I am merely honest. Far more so than young men who make promises and then break them. If you stay on the Isle de Luc, I can't promise to make you glad you stayed. It is up to you, Kara. Take a chance, but be warned that you can't turn the tide, or change the leopard's markings.'

A silence fell between them, and then he let his hand touch her shoulder and drift to her wrist, where he fingered the little unicorn on her wrist-chain. He examined the unicorn.

'Creature of myth,' he murmured. 'Like yourself, Kara, with your face that one might see peering through leaves in a woodland.'

She felt his touch, and the acute sensitivity of her own skin. She drew her wrist away from his fingers, and it was an effort, as though she fought a magnetism in them.

'The hotel is quiet—everyone must be asleep,' she said. 'I bid you *kale nichta*, Mr. Savidge.'

'Good night, Miss Stephanos.' As he drew away, the wall light struck across the whip scar on his cheekbone, and then he gave her a faintly mocking bow that revealed the Gallic blood in him . . . from the mother who had marked him as Cain.

CHAPTER THREE

KARA had been on the Isle de Luc almost a week, and on Friday morning she slipped out of the hotel alone and made her way to the waterfront market, where she hoped the bustle would divert her thoughts for a while.

She wandered about, a seemingly carefree young figure in a sea-island shirt and trews, amused by the market mammies in big straw hats perched raffishly on bright bandanas, presiding over piles of island fruits and vegetables. There was a tang of spices and coffee beans, sea-wet quay stones, and salt fish.

Men of the sea, with high-boned faces and voices rich as dark honey, were unloading boat loads of conch in the shell, crawling lobsters, and red snapper. Huge primitive masks were on sale beside leaning towers of straw hats, and fetishes. Kara stroked the shiny carapace of a turtle, and listened to the excited talk aroused by the carnival that was taking place the following day, when out would come the masks, the drums, and the satyrs who collected money for various charities.

There would be turtle feasts around drift-wood fires down on the beach. The people of Fort Fernand would go on the spree for a day and a night, and couples would fall in and out of love.

'You like funny-face nut?' A big brown hand thrust a coconut at Kara, who asked laughingly that it be cut open. The young Negro swung a cutlass that lopped off the top of the nut and with a dazzling grin he handed Kara the cup of milk. She tipped the cup and drank. The milk was icy, with a tang of the sea in it.

'*Merci.*' She smiled at so sweet a bribe, and obligingly took a look at the carnival favours the young man was selling. She bought a string of beads made from coloured seeds, and couldn't resist a frilled mask of polka-dot silk.

'This one ver' fierce. You like?'

'No,' Kara said, and then took another look. It was of dark crimson and would fit a man to the mouth. Kara took hold of it and pictured the mask half covering the face of Lucan Savidge, his lips beneath it curling into the smile that was so devilish at times.

'You buy?'

'Yes.' She smiled, and then caught her bottom lip between her teeth. How would Lucan react to the mask, would he wear it for the carnival, or scorn it? There was no telling. After almost a week she was still unsure with him, like a small girl who bears constantly in mind the warning that it is dangerous to try and touch the leopard through the bars of his cage.

She wandered on, the beads around her neck and the masks in her shoulder-strap bag. People bellowed and bargained and laughed richly, and over all hung the smells of firestick coffee, brown sugar, ginger cookies, and tropical fruits bursting with a lush ripeness.

The turbulence of the old days still lingered in Fort Fernand. The overhanging *galeries* of the side-street houses seemed haunted by the Creole beauties of long ago, clad in flame skirts and frilled blouses, big hooped earrings glittering beneath horned turbans. The town was time-weathered, its scars concealed by masses of bougainvillea. And there was the old slave-square, where jungle warriors were handled long ago like cattle, and lithe brown girls were sold to the merchants and the plantocrats.

Kara tried to imagine what it must have been like to be a slave, the possession of a man who cared nothing about your feelings. If you rebelled, you were whipped. If you ran away, you were hunted by big black dogs let loose in

54

the cane fields and the forests. Awful, unimaginable, and Kara hurried from her thoughts down a sloping, cobbled street that led to the shore, where shrimping boats lay on their sides, draped with fishing nets.

The scene was almost Greek, and Kara thought of the long letter she had written yesterday to Paul and Domini, describing all she had so far seen of the Isle de Luc—but she had not mentioned Lucan Savidge.

She had a feeling that Paul—with his business contacts in most parts of the world—would make inquiries about the Savidges of Dragon Bay, and that what he learned would not be to his liking.

Kara sat down on the side of one of the shrimping boats, and her fingers played nervously with her string of coloured beads. She adored her brother Paul, and never before had she kept anything from him—but her friendship with Lucan Savidge was something she didn't want to write about, or think about. In a few days she and Lucan would say good-bye. He would return to Dragon Bay, and she would continue with her tour of the Caribbean. This strange interlude on the Isle de Luc would be over, and Lucan would be but a memory. . . .

'Oh—!' The exclamation broke from Kara

as her necklace suddenly broke and the beads scattered and rolled to the sands. She knelt and began to pick up the beads, as distressed as if she had broken a string of pearls. The beads were a memento of her visit to the Isle de Luc, their value lay in their future ability to bring back vividly to her senses all the colour and vitality of the waterfront market this morning, and the Creole houses.

She was absorbed in her rescue work when someone leapt the sea-wall and came loping down the sands to where she was on her knees. A large pair of sandalled feet planted themselves in front of her, and she glanced up startled at the tall figure in a matelot shirt and slacks, his hair sun-fired above amused green eyes.

''Tis a big girl ye are for shell hunting,' he said in a mock Irish brogue.

'I—I broke a string of beads.' Her earlobes tingled and gave warning of a blush, and she jumped quickly to her feet and thrust the handful of beads into her jacket pocket. 'How did you know where I was?' she asked diffidently.

'A market mammy saw you crossing the old slave-square, and I guessed you would make for the shore. Why did you slip out alone?'

'Because I wanted to be alone.' The words

56

slipped out before she could stop them, and she and Lucan stared at one another, the sea behind them awash with gold from the sun. The palms bowed gently, and small bright birds fluttered in the green crests.

'There are two kinds of women so honest, Kara, the artless, and the heartless. I know which you are—here, catch!' he tossed something and she caught it with the dexterity of a girl who had been a tomboy. It was a mammy apple, whose fruit had the mixed tartness and sweetness of an apricot.

'Do you know what the islanders say about this fruit?' His teeth were white against his tanned skin as he took a bite of his own mammy apple. 'They say it is the forbidden fruit that Eve gave to Adam to tempt him.'

'Are you reversing the procedure and trying to tempt me?' Kara's voice was lighter than her spirit, which felt curiously weighed down. Come carnival time, come Sunday, and Lucan would take a raft out of her life. That was why she had come out alone this morning, to see how it felt to be alone after almost a week of swimming with Lucan, of touring Fort Fernand by his side, and dining at colourful places in the evening and being held in his arms when they danced.

The attraction she felt could not be love.

She told herself with panic in her heart that she loved Nikos. She had loved him all her life, and it was hurt pride that made another man seem so terribly attractive. . . .

'Would you like me to tempt you?'

'Yes, to breakfast.' She darted away from him, up the sloping shore to the sea-wall. She scrambled over and with the wall between them laughed at him, the sun catching the tiny rings in her earlobes. 'Let us go and eat at that little place like a *kafenion*.'

'Are you homesick for Greece?' With a lithe bound Lucan was beside her and they began to walk up the cobbled street to the town.

'I miss my second love, my Dominic.' She felt the flick of green eyes. 'He will be three in June.'

'And this is May,' drawled Lucan. 'The cane is young and green at Dragon Bay, and the cocoa valley is rich with spicy scents and cool with shadows.'

'You sound homesick yourself,' said Kara, and when she glanced at him she saw the look he had, a flare to his nostrils as though he took a deep, imaginary breath of the scents in the cocoa valley.

'I suppose I am,' he admitted. 'The need to get away is never as strong as the urge to get home again. I've been to France—to visit a friend.'

His voice seemed to linger on that final word, and Kara wondered if he meant a woman. She thought it more than likely, for this was a man who was alive from his fiery crest of hair to the soles of his feet, with the look of ancient Ireland when chariots thundered over the ruts of the wild roads, and harps played in the smoky halls of Tara, where the warrior princes and chieftains gathered.

'Here we are.' She felt his hand rest lightly on her waist as they paused outside the little harbour restaurant that looked so much like a Greek coffee-shop, with its sun-faded tables and chairs set out under an arbour of vines.

They chose a table near a mass of pink pandoras, and ordered langouste caught in the surf that morning, brown bread, lashings of butter, and big cups of island coffee.

'I am hungry.' Kara clasped her hands on the table top and blinked her dark lashes as a shaft of sunlight cut between her and Lucan like a blade. He leant to one side, plucked a pandora blossom and handed it to her with a sideways smile that mocked the gesture even as he made it.

'Pandora,' she murmured, stroking the petals, 'why did you give your husband your wedding casket, so he could let out all the tears and troubles it contained, and then shut the lid on hope?'

'You are an odd child.' Lucan was gazing across at her, a half amused glint in his eyes— green this morning as the Greek sky at evening time.

'I daresay I am different from the chic sophisticates you must be used to,' she said lightly. 'I hope I don't bore you?'

'If you did that, you wouldn't be sitting here with me,' he said flatly. 'I don't roam around with you, telling you all the old Creole stories of this island because I'm kind, Kara. Because you're a stranger nursing a bit of heartache. What do I care about your heartache—not that!' He snapped his fingers. 'You happen to intrigue me. You're a little Greek riddle I can't quite fathom—there, does that satisfy your curiosity about why I bother with you?'

'I never thought you kind,' she said quietly, 'so why I bother with you is a mystery to me.'

'*Touché*,' he laughed. 'It's that bit of spirit, and those eyes like peaty pools on an Irish moor that I like, Kara. The blush, too, and the fingernails curling and wanting to dagger my cheek.'

She whipped her hand off the table and the

pandora blossom fell to the ground. She let it lie there. She didn't want his flower, nor his careless Irish compliments. She wished the week-end was over. Wished she had the courage to walk away now and deny herself these last few days of his tormenting company.

'Our *langouste*,' he drawled, and as the waiter unloaded his tray on to their table, Kara saw Lucan finger the whip-scar on his cheek and smile cynically. Her heart beat like the hidden wings of the cicadas. To her dismay she wanted to pull his hand away from the mark and shield it with a kiss!

* * *

The carnival spirit was infectious, and Kara asked Nap to take her to a shop where she could hire a fancy dress. She wanted to surprise Lucan—to stun him, if possible—and was delighted to be able to hire a real Creole costume complete with a *madras*, a winged turban of bright silk, and hoops for her ears.

She wanted the costume for the *bal masqué* that was being held in the gardens of the most imposing old house in Fort Fernand. Lucan Savidge knew the people who were giving the party, and he had casually invited Kara to go with him. 'It's a costume ball and you can hire something to wear—if you fancy to go.'

'Why not?' she said, feeling a pulse leap of excitement. 'It will be something to remember, a *bal masqué* at carnival time on the Isle de Luc. Will you wear a fancy costume, Lucan?'

'What shall I wear, the guise of a corsair?' Through the smoke of his Gauloise his eyes had gleamed with diablerie.

'Let us surprise one another,' she said eagerly.

By ten o'clock the following morning, Fort Fernand was in the first throes of carnival. The narrow streets were thronged with people, some already in costume, others dressed in starched white suits and dazzling cotton dresses. The sun shone down on ebony and coffee faces. The pigtails of the little girls stood out from their eager faces, while small boys dashed hither and thither with balloons blown up into flying geese, clowns and animal shapes.

The rich clamour of voices rose to the front balconies of the Hotel Victoire, crammed with a sudden influx of guests from the interior of the island. Wealthy planters and their families, who chattered in Creole as they awaited the decorated floats, the carnival queen's chariot, and the motley of islanders clad in costumes depicting their colourful history.

Kara was only half aware of the inquisitive glances cast in her direction by the nearby girls who were going to the *bal masqué* that evening. They giggled and talked together in voices too low to be clearly heard, and then Lucan pushed his way to Kara's side and the girlish chatter died away into a sudden hush.

The gay spectacle below held Kara's attention, and then she felt Lucan's hand crushing hers on the balcony rail. 'My poor hand,' she glanced up at him with a laughing gasp. 'You are mangling it!'

'Forgive me.' His face was curiously hard, though his fingers lost their tension. 'Do you understand Creole?' he asked quietly.

'Only if I listen carefully. Why?' She noticed that his eyes were diamond-grey, which meant that he was angry about something. 'Look at the crowds, Lucan. I had no idea there were so many people on this small island.'

'Enough, and sometimes too many.' He cast an ironical glance around the crowded balcony. 'Shall we go down to the street to watch the Grand Parade?'

'If you would like to.' She spoke eagerly,

and was aware as she followed Lucan of a rather chilly silence. She realized with a pang that these people had been whispering about her and Lucan!

He was smiling ruefully when they reached the street. 'I've made a scarlet woman of you, Kara,' he said. 'Do you mind?'

'Do I look as though I mind?' She gave him a quick smile, a gamine figure with her dark hair flowing and her cheeks flushed. 'Lucan, I hear the drums! The carnival has begun!'

Excitement ran through the crowds as the thud and boom of the drums drew closer and the carnival dragons came into view, swaying above a float on which a miniature sugar mill puffed smoke, followed by another on which colourfully clad 'slaves' danced around a great cauldron in which a girl sat on a mound of sugar.

Appreciative laughter swept the crowd, and they cheered as a flower float rumbled by, filled with pretty girls and masses of tropical flowers. Came the tall black satyrs with their money-nets, hooking people with their tridents and demanding a forfeit in cash for charity. Kara got hooked, and Lucan threw a handful of silver into the stayr's net. 'You bought that gal, suh,' someone laughed, and as Lucan jestingly tossed her to his shoulder, there ran through Kara a sensation that melted her bones and shook her heart.

'Put me down, Lucan!' In the strangest panic she pummelled his broad shoulders. 'Please—everyone is looking!'

With a flash of his teeth and a laugh, he slid her down the long length of his body to the ground. 'Behave yourself, slave,' he was looking down deep into her confused eyes, 'or I won't buy you a pineapple.'

A vendor was selling them from a basket, green-plumed, golden with plump fruit and juice. Lucan had a large one quartered, and never had fruit tasted so delicious to Kara, enjoyed in the midst of the carnival crowds on a Caribbean island. There was a strange new magic to being alive and among these vital people; noisy, sunlit hours Kara relished to the full.

Boom, clash, boom. Cymbals caught the sun on their blades, and tom-toms throbbed as a parade of costumed islanders followed the chariot of the carnival queen. Voodoo dancers, slave maidens, Aztec warriors, and temple devils.

As the carnival moved on, the crowd followed it through the narrow streets, where the balconies were bright with flowers and holidaymakers. Streamers tangled people together, and great clown heads wagged and wobbled high overhead. Confetti showered down from burst balloons, and it was all over Kara's hair and Lucan's fiery mane as they were swept along with the laughing, sweating, flirting tide of people.

It was some time later when Lucan pulled Kara into a doorway to catch their breath. The noise and the music gradually died away, and Kara leaned back against the sun-scaled door, a tousled, dusty figure with streamers wrapped around her and confetti in her hair. 'Mad, all quite mad,' she laughed breathlessly, 'but I would not have missed a moment of it.'

'Let me unbind you.' Lucan's face was creased with amusement, his eyes as green as Irish moss as he unwound the streamers and released her from their gay bondage.

'Thank you.' Kara gazed at him and remembered how the queen of the carnival had thrown him a flower from her bouquet. He had caught it deftly, and a smile had run all over the girl's piquant face beneath her crown. A creamy heart of a face with an underlying hint of coffee, eyes like pools of honey, and a mouth like a wine-coloured flower.

Was the girl known to him, Kara wondered, or had she noticed how he stood out in the crowd?

'Where is the flower the carnival queen deigned to toss you?' she asked with a smile.

'I stuck it behind the pigtail of a piccaninny,' he said half mockingly. 'Jealous?'

'No.' Kara combed the confetti out of her hair with her fingers. 'Monkey was always my nickname when I was a child, and if I was ever jealous of anyone it was of Domini, my brother's wife. But not for long did my jealousy last. Domini has a heart to match her lovely face.'

'Domini is a rare and lovely name.' Lucan thumbed his lighter and fired a cheroot. Smoke drifted lazily from his nostrils.

'Domini is a rare and lovely person,' Kara said softly. 'When you love a brother with all your heart, you can not imagine a woman good enough for him, or spirited enough. Paul fought for Greece when he was a boy, and he was desperately hurt. He almost died of that injury five years ago ... Domini held him back with her love. She defied the gods who take young those they love, and my dear Apollo did not die, nor was he blinded as he desperately feared he would be. He has the use of one of his eyes—and with it he misses 'very little,' Kara ended, half laughing, a rather choked sound.

'Paul, dearest brother,' she thought, 'I ran away from Andelos because my pride was hurt, and I have run into a man you would perhaps not like—not at first. What I felt for Nikos was never like this feeling I have for Lucan Savidge. I don't know if it is love, but I do know that parting from him, tomorrow or the day after, will be hard to bear.'

'Let us go and swim,' Lucan suggested. 'We can buy bathing wear from that shop down by the harbour, and food for a beach picnic. It will save a return trip to the hotel.'

'*Ne, kyrie.*' She spoke in her own tongue because she had been thinking in Greek.

'Are you saying no to me, young lady?' Lucan quirked an eyebrow.

'A Greek yes always sounds a little like a no,' she explained.

'I must remember that,' he smiled, wickedly.

Everyone was at the carnival and they had the beach to themselves. The sea was like a mass of melted emeralds in motion, and they made for the shade of some large rocks to which sea-grape clung, and laid out the rug and the picnic basket which Lucan had hired. Kara, eager to get into the water, ran behind

68

the rocks to change into her swim-suit, a one-piece suit whose straps were very white against her skin that the Greek sun had turned golden long ago. She ran out from the sheltering rocks and down towards the sea.

'Slow boat!' she tossed over her shoulder, and in an instant Lucan was racing after her. She cried out as she felt the warm snatch of his arms, lifting her as easily as if she were sea-drift.

'Y-you brigand—!' She twisted and wriggled in his arms, but could not escape, and laughing and merciless he tossed her into the buoyant water of the Caribbean; water as clear as a green jewel, warm on the surface, with cooler depths.

Green . . . green as Lucan's eyes, drowning her for an instant of time, then letting her surface, breathless. Lucan swam around her in a circle, sleek as a sea-tiger, showing his white teeth in a mocking smile.

'You wretch!' she half laughed, and with easy strokes she swam away from him, silk-sheathed by the water and tensely aware of the man who dived beneath her, whose companionship in and out of the sea had a tingling edge of danger to it.

Kara was the first out of the water, shaking her hair like a puppy and letting the hot sun dry the sea-water to a salty bloom on her limbs. What an ocean! Fish as bright as butterflies swam in and out of coral honeycombs, ferns of jade, crimson and bronze waved underwater, and sea-anemones spread their petals at the touch of a toe and revealed their hearts.

Kara sighed and stretched her arms to the sun. She was Greek and she worshipped nature in all its wild loveliness. Her toes curled into the warm sand as Lucan came out of the sea, his brown lance of a body dripping off the water in which he was at home as a pearl pirate.

'That was good.' He put back his head and seemed to swallow the sun in greedy gulps. 'Kara, you swim like a boy.'

'So I have been told before.' Too often, she thought, as she made for the picnic basket. She knelt and opened the basket and took a look at the food inside. A whole roast chicken, tomatoes and slices of pumpkin. A coconut and lemon pie. A bottle of wine—but no glasses or cups!

Lucan threw himself down beside her and

70

for a tingling moment she felt his fingers ruffling her hair—as though she were a puppy. 'Bad management,' she said pertly. 'We have wine, Lucan, but no glasses.'

'Then we shall have to drink from the bottle—like pirates.' His fingers touched the furrow of innocence at the nape of her neck, and she stiffened. 'Afraid of any man's touch—or just mine?' he murmured.

'Having been thrown into the sea, and as unmercifully chased as if by a tiger shark, I am wary of your intentions, Mr. Savidge.' She pulled paper plates and tomatoes out of the food basket, and hoped she didn't look as defenceless as she felt with Lucan so close, teasing her with his green-devil eyes, and being curious about her in relation to other men. There had been only Nikos, and he had never kissed her with passion. Innocent, unawakened, she had not known until now that unless there was passion, there was only affection.

'Let me calm your nerves with a little music.' He began to fiddle with the miniradio, which he had bought as casually as the swimsuit she was wearing, and her beach hat of conical straw. He adjusted the aerial and to the beat of a calypso they tore the cold roast chicken apart and ate hungrily. The wine tasted heady straight from the mouth of the bottle . . . from Lucan's lips.

The trade winds blew softly and rustled the handshaped leaves of the palm trees, and the surf lapped the pebbles at the edge of the sands. 'Mmm, delicious pumpkin.' Kara ate a slice, her eyes wine-drowsy as she took in the idyllic scene, and the warm vibrancy of Lucan's hair in the sun.

The radio music changed, and now there was a jungle beat in it.

'Do you swim often at Dragon Bay?' Kara asked.

'Sometimes early in the morning, or at night under the stars.' He stretched out, replete, the tropical sun and sea absorbed through all the hard bone and sinew of him. 'There are barracuda in our waters, and the breakers run high. The rocks are like dragon's teeth, and there is an undertow like the grip of a monster tail.'

'The place hardly sounds like a holiday resort.' Kara cradled her updrawn knees with her arms, her straw hat tipped over her nose, shielding her eyes and her interest in Lucan's home which was a day's trip by river to the other side of the Isle de Luc where there were stretches of wild coastline.

'It takes strong people to live at Dragon

Bay,' he said. 'The strong—and the ruthless.'

'How did it come by the name of Dragon Bay?' She tried to speak casually, afraid that he would guess that her interest was not casual.

'Our crest is a scarlet dragon crouched on a bronze shield. Our family motto declares that the Savidge Dragon Guards His Own.' Kara could feel Lucan looking at her with narrowed eyes beneath a crest of hair as bronze as an Irish war-shield. 'On the mantel in the hall of the Great House stands a golden drinking-cup inlaid with a scarlet dragon which the rebel Savidges—two brothers—brought with them from Ireland. Like all Irishmen they had hearts full of pride and a devil or two, and they were not accepting the bondage of the English. They caused quite a bit of havoc, and then with the soldiers after them they boarded a ship that was sailing for the Caribbean.

'That ship ran on to the rocks off the north side of this island. The brothers managed to swim ashore, and with them a girl called Maeve, and a dozen Caribs whom the Captain had picked up on the way—to be sold as slaves. Conal and Diarmuid saw how good the soil was above the bay, and they pledged the golden drinking-cup for a piece of land and with the Caribs working for them they planted their first sugar crop. Conal married the girl Maeve, and when the time came for building a house, the brothers set it high above the waters in which they had nearly drowned, and they named the bay after the Savidge dragon.'

'What of Diarmuid, did he not marry?' Kara asked.

'He was married to the plantations, and he left Conal to found the Caribbean branch of the Savidge family. Maeve died, carrying her fourth child, from a fall down the cliff steps to the bay. Later on another Savidge bride died in the sugar mill when it caught fire. The Savidge dragon seems to bear a grudge against the Savidge brides.'

Kara gave a shiver in the sun, for Lucan had evoked with Irish imagery the atmosphere at Dragon Bay—strange and brooding; the breakers crashing over the rocks, loud enough to drown the screams of Maeve when she had fallen down the cliff steps long, long ago.

Pryde had fallen, too.

'Oh, Lucan, look!' Kara pointed at a crab that was waddling along in a shell that was obviously a cast-off. They laughed together at the comical sight, and then their laughter died away, and Kara's eyes were made captive by Lucan's. The sea whispered and the hands of the palm trees beckoned, and then his hands found her and she was pulled down across his sun-hot chest. She fought with him, but his lean body was full of a strength that made struggling with him a breathless futility.

'Don't do this,' she begged.

'What am I going to do?' he drawled.

'Spoil our friendship.'

'Little fool, is that what it is?' His arms tightened, then the world spun over and the sand was beneath her and Lucan's mouth was crushing hers.

He kissed her as if he wanted to drown out thought, and then he drew away from her and she lay with closed eyes, her mouth wounded by the kiss that had held no tenderness. She trembled as he brushed his lips savagely across her throat.

'For the love of Lucifer!' His thumb flicked off the tear that rolled down her cheek. 'Did it hurt that much—did that boy-friend of yours never kiss you?'

'Not like that,' she choked. 'Nikos is not a rough person.'

'Then your Nikos is not yet a man. Faith, do you have to cry?'

'Y-you don't like to see a woman cry

because you are cruel.'

'What a paradox!' he mocked.

'It's true. A few tears might touch you, and you are not going to allow that to happen.'

'I am so formidable?'

Her wet eyes opened and she lay beneath the spread of his shoulders as though thrown to the sand by a corsair. His foxfire hair was rough from the sea and tousled. His eyes leapt green and dangerous. His hard body was without a bone of tenderness, brown from the sun and wind and wild waters of Dragon Bay.

'You are the most complicated person I have ever known, Lucan,' she said. 'I— don't think I like you very much.'

'Did I ask you to like me, Kara? Did I give the impression that I needed a—friend?' He was laughing as he pulled her to her feet and brushed the sand grains from her shoulders. His fingertips were slightly rasping, so that when something less rasping touched her shoulder she knew it to be his lips. So briefly, a flame that came and went.

'What are you thinking?' He stood in front of her and blocked out the green churning of the sea.

'What do you want of me?' she asked.

He tipped her chin with his forefinger and studied her face with eyes gone from green to grey. 'Does tradition mean anything to you, Kara?'

'Tradition?' She gazed up at him, perplexed.

'The Savidge tradition has come to mean less to me than it used to, but my brother sets great store by it—and I set great store by my brother.'

'I can understand the love for a brother,' she said simply.

'But you don't understand me? I confound you, eh?'

'Too much—' She pulled away from him and knelt to pack up their picnic. She shook out the rug and folded it, and the music died away as he switched off the little radio. Kara went behind the rocks to dress, and when she came out Lucan had pulled on his slacks and was sliding his T-shirt down over his brown chest. His head emerged, and she saw that he was looking taut-featured and withdrawn.

A glow was spreading over the sea, as though fire was licking out of the horizon, and when Kara and Lucan reached the end of the harbour they turned in unison to gaze back at the pagan wonder of the sunset, the sea aflame, crimson and gold, and the crests of the palms etched against the glow.

By the time they reached the hotel, thousands of lanterns had blazed alight in the streets. Laughing groups of people clustered around the food stalls, and tangled balls of streamers and confetti lay underfoot. There was a low throbbing of tom-toms stealing out of the dark . . . excitement held its breath until the moment when the masked dancing would begin.

Then the Harlequins would leap, the drums would pound, and Fort Fernand would be as it was in the past—barbaric and gay, everyone living for the moment, loving tonight and paying the cost tomorrow.

★   ★   ★

Kara stood in front of the mirror in her hotel bedroom and gazed at the reflection of a stranger. A petite stranger in a full panniered skirt of flowered silk over a froth of petticoats. Her waist looked tiny enough to be spanned by a pair of hands, and the creamy fichu of her blouse was fastened with a little golden lyre. Her winged headdress and Creole earrings intensified the Byzantine shape of her eyes, and excitement flushed her lips and trembled at the edges of them.

'Kara Stephanos, you look almost pretty.'

She curtsied at her reflection and laughed. 'Domini and Paul would be proud if they could see you—'

She caught her breath. What sort of an impression would she make on Lucan, who had kissed her on the beach that afternoon and spoken so strangely about his home and the Savidge tradition?

The memory of his kiss, of being at his mercy in his hard brown arms, was so vivid that she could almost feel his lips again and her heart's invasion by his heartbeats.

With a rustle of silk and lace she turned away from her mirrored eyes, and her hands trembled as she toyed with the mask she had bought yesterday. To a man like Lucan a kiss did not signify anything beyond mere gratification of the moment—or a desire to see how she reacted. She must remember that at the *bal masqué* tonight. The music, the masks, and the moonlight could go to all heads but hers.

She was adjusting her mask when there was a knock on her door. She knew at once that it was Lucan, and for a wild moment she thought of saying she had a headache and felt unable to go to the ball. But when she reached the door and opened it, she was lost for words. She could only gaze at him

79

through the openings of her mask.

He leaned against the wall in a nonchalant attitude, and he wore the motley of Harlequin.

Silently she handed him the mask she had promised him but before putting it on he appraised her from her winged 'madras' to the tips of her dancing slippers, peeping from the hem of her frilly skirt.

'You look charming, *petite*.' His smile flashed wickedly. '*La dame Creole* in all her glory.'

'Thank you.' She watched him adjust the crimson mask; it fitted perfectly over his brow and his blade of a nose, and she drew back against the jamb of the door as in front of her eyes the man became a devil.

'Well?' he drawled. 'Will I do?'

'You will frighten every girl at the ball,' Kara said, with a laughing gasp.

'As long as I don't frighten you.' He leaned forward and his eyes glinted with secret laughter through the slits of his mask. 'Do I frighten you, Kara?'

'Sometimes,' she admitted. 'You are right to wear motley, for who knows Lucan Savidge knows only one side of him?'

'What do you know, little one?'

Her heart skipped a beat at the casual

endearment. 'That all the girls you have known mean less to you than the spindrift that flies over the rocks at Dragon Bay,' she replied. 'When you talk of your home you have a savage ring of love in your voice that no woman could put there, and I pity the woman you will take there one day as your wife.'

His eyes glinted through his mask as he heard her out, then he straightened to his full, dominating height. 'Shall we be off to the ball?' was all he said.

She swished in her silk and lace as she went down the stairs by his side. When they reached the lobby a party of costumed merry-makers were emerging from the lift. They were bound for the *bal masqué* and the men of the party greeted Lucan with reserve and gave Kara the coolest of bows.

She hardly cared what these people thought. She had already guessed that they had heard of the night she had spent in Lucan's bedroom. That it had been entirely innocent would not occur to them. Any girl in Lucan Savidge's bedroom was bound to be a *coquette*.

'Are you going to the ball, Miss Stephanos?' One of the young women was gazing at Kara with a look of avid curiosity in her

81

eyes. She wore eighteenth-century costume with a powdered wig and beauty patches, and there was something of Paris chic about her, as though she might be a guest at one of the plantations instead of a resident.

Kara nodded coolly, unprepared to be sociable with people who treated Lucan as a rake.

'We must have a little talk later on,' said the girl, and a cold finger seemed to touch Kara's heart as she followed Lucan out of the hotel.

'Do you know her?' Lucan asked, as he handed her into the open carriage young Nap had secured for them. She shook her head, and then forgot the incident as they made slow progress through the noisy streets and up the cobbled hill to the French-Colonial house where the ball was taking place.

*   *   *

A big open pavilion in the gardens had been turned into a ballroom, and as this was a *bal masqué* the music was old-fashioned and romantic. Masked couples could be seen whirling to the music through tall arched openings of the circular pavilion, and ceiling lanterns sparkled and threw jewel colours down upon the colourful throng.

Kara's heart quickened with excitement as she and Lucan stepped through one of the archways. She turned and smiled up at him, one of several Harlequins but like no other because of his height and his crimson mask. She entered his arms and felt them tighten as they danced.

The melody was *Lilac Domino*, and Kara closed her eyes as she gave herself up to the music and tried to recapture the carefree pleasure of another time, another place, and the arms of Nikos. But no, those moments could not be recalled in Lucan's arms. His personality was too strong.

She felt herself drawn close to his hard body as they whirled round and round at the climax of the waltz. She seemed to melt, to become part of his motley. *No, no*, cried her heart. This is a dark enchantment, not love. This time your heart will be broken, not merely bruised!

The music died, the spell was broken, and he was pulling her by the hand to where the buffet was laid. They ate crab legs and shrimps dipped in a delectable sauce, and drank champagne. His teeth flashed in laughter below his crimson mask, and Kara was aware all the time of feminine eyes upon him.

Some shone boldly through the mask openings, others looked at him with a fascination verging on fear.

The queen of the carnival was at the ball, looking picturesque in a brilliantly coloured Martinique costume. Later on, Lucan said casually, she would send one of her pages to the man she desired to have the *Empress Waltz* with. This was all part of the annual fun and games.

Kara watched the bubbles rising to the rim of her champagne glass. 'You are looking into your wine glass as though into a fortune-teller's crystal,' Lucan laughed.

'Shall I make a prediction?' Kara slanted him an impish smile.

'No, come and dance,' he said, and he took the glass out of her hand and put it down on the buffet table, and the next moment they were in among the crush of dancers. It was then that Kara glimpsed the French-woman who had spoken to her in the lobby of the hotel, and again she stared at Kara—most disapprovingly—as their partners swept them past each other. Kara looked away from her, reminded uncomfortably of a girl she had known at school, who was always ready at the slightest broken rule to say: 'I'll tell on you, Kara.'

'Who is the girl in the powdered wig and patches?' Lucan was looking down at her. 'She seems to know you, Kara.'

'I don't know her.' Kara tilted her chin to look at him. 'People have been talking about us, Lucan, and she is evidently curious about me.'

'I am afraid the Isle de Luc is a small enough place for any gossip to grow out of proportion.' His teeth glinted below his mask. Do you mind being thought Lucan Savidge's latest jade?'

'Have there been many, Lucan?'

'What do you think?'

'That you don't care much what I think.'

'Then let us leave it at that.' They executed a movement in the foxtrot they were dancing and she felt his grip tighten on her fingers until the bones ached, then his grip relaxed and she wondered whether he hurt her for being right about him, or wrong.

The gaiety increased as the hours slipped by. Big coloured balloons and balls of streamers were let down from a net in the ceiling, and the fun was at its height when it was announced that the carnival queen would now choose her partner for the *Empress Waltz*. A buzz of speculation swept round the pavilion as the lovely girl in her colourful flounces bent to whisper in the ear of one of her pages in yellow silk. The boy nodded and with a look of great importance on his pert brown face he began to thread his way through the gay crowd thronging the verge of the dance floor.

Kara watched that small figure in a yellow tunic and knee-breeches, the buckles twinkling on his shoes, as he drew nearer all the time to where she stood beside the tallest Harlequin in that big, warm, scented pavilion . . . all talk hushed as the page tapped Lucan on the arm.

He bowed in the carnival queen's direction, then he turned to Kara and his eyes gleamed through the slits of his crimson mask. 'Will you excuse me?' he drawled. 'It would be inexcusable if I refused to dance with the prettiest girl on the Isle de Luc.'

'I am sure it would,' Kara smiled, for she had known all along that the carnival queen would choose Lucan as her partner. 'I hope you enjoy yourself.'

'I shall,' he said, and the next moment he was striding across the dance floor towards the girl whose wisp of a mask did not hide the dimples of satisfaction in her creamy cheeks. A murmur swept around the crowded pavilion as to the opening bars of the waltz,

86

Lucan drew the charming girl into his arms and whirled her on to the dance floor with the authority and assurance of a king.

They waltzed alone until they had circled the floor, and then one by one they were joined by other couples until the floor was a moving sea of colour and eyes sparkling through mask openings.

Kara drew back into the shadows beyond the dance floor, and then she bunched her skirts in her hands and ran out into the garden. She told herself she did not care that Lucan danced with a beautiful girl, but her heart was heavy as she walked among the whispering trees and breathed the peachy scent of frangipani.

She began to follow the scent, and suddenly a cold little thrill ran through her as she heard someone brush through the trees behind her. She swung round as a hand parted the hangings of a monkey-tail tree and an eighteenth-century figure stepped in front of her.

'If a man did that to *me* I would never talk to him again.' It was the woman in the powdered wig and patches who confronted Kara in a beam of moonlight. 'I followed you to have a little talk with you.

'I resent being spied upon and followed,' Kara said, her voice sharp with dislike. 'Who are you?'

'A friend of Paul and Domini Stephanos.'

Kara stifled a little cry of surprise, and distress.

'Such a small world, is it not?' The woman had unmasked and the moonlight gleamed down on her rather cold features and thin, painted lips. 'From the moment someone told me your name and that you were Greek, I knew that you were the young stepsister of Paul Stephanos, whom I met in Paris last year with his lovely wife Domini. I met them at the Louvre. I was there with a friend, and it turned out that he and your brother knew each other. The four of us dined at Maxim's that evening and had a wonderful time. Paul talked so fluently of Andelos and its colourful and old-fashioned customs.'

The moonlight shone on satin as the woman drew nearer to Kara. She raised her left hand and fingered a beauty patch on her cheekbone. Her hand flaunted a large, square-cut diamond, but the ring was a dress-ring and not on the finger that would have proclaimed her the beloved of a man, who might have softened that cold face and put warmth in those basilisk eyes.

'What a splendid man your brother is.' The thin lips smiled . . . a flicker, as of a snake striking. 'So *proud*—I really must write to Domini and tell her of our meeting—she will be so surprised, eh?'

Again those cold fingers curled about Kara's heart. This woman with the bitter-sweet smile was a troublemaker. There was spite in her heart because never had she been loved by a man like Paul . . . or wanted by a man like Lucan.

'You know, my dear, you hardly look the sort to have affairs, and hardly the type to attract Lucan Savidge.' She gave a malicious laugh that was echoed by the tinkling coo of a bird among the trees. 'Could you not bear to see him dancing with that exquisite creature in there? Is that why you ran out into the night?'

'Lucan and I are friends and nothing more,' Kara spoke with Greek dignity, 'and if you write anything to my brother that robs me, or Lucan, of our good name—'

'What good name has Lucan Savidge?' the woman asked scornfully. 'Everyone on this island knows that his brother is in a wheelchair because of him—that if Pryde had been killed, Lucan would be the master at Dragon Bay.'

'Lucan was not responsible for that accident,' Kara defended him, fiercely. 'He told

89

me himself that it was Pryde who suggested they climb the cliff that rises steep from the bay—'

'*He* told you?' Thin dark eyebrows rose to meet the silvery wig. 'Do you in your innocence believe everything that *he* tells you? The Da at the Great House—Nanny to the boys from their birth—heard Lucan challenge his brother to the climb. She told their mother so after the accident, and she would hardly make up such a story. Poor Pryde was too ill and broken to be able to deny or support whatever Lucan said, and when he began to recover his senses he could not remember who had been the one to make the challenge. Most convenient for Lucan, enabling him to act the martyr with silly little girls who can't see beyond his green eyes to the ambitious animal that stalks inside his tawny skin.'

'You talk about Lucan Savidge as though you hate him,' Kara said. 'What has he ever done to you?'

'Why, nothing.' The woman's laugh was metallic. 'I know him by repute, and I abhor his type. Women are nothing but playthings to such men—and the playthings are usually brainless dolls. You really are the exception, Kara.'

'Lucan is a friend and nothing more—'

'My dear, it must be a very *close* friendship, from all accounts.' And with a sharp rustle of satin the woman swung about and walked quickly away, leaving Kara alone among the trees. She gave a shiver as a click-beetle darted past her cheek, flickering green as the twisted envy of the girl in the silver wig. She was no friend of Paul or Domini, but someone who needed to hurt those who were in love and happy. She would write her letter because of that, and Kara would have no antidote against its poison because the man into whose room she had wandered was Lucan Savidge.

Kara glanced about her, feeling like someone lost in a bad dream. Music stole through the trees, reminding her of the *bal masqué* and the gaiety; and of Lucan holding in his arms the queen of the ball. Kara knew she ought to go back to the pavilion, but instead she followed the scent of the frangipani. Her polka-dot mask fell unnoticed from her hand, and in a while she came to a little pagoda wreathed in the coral stars of the temple flower that evoked memories of the first evening she had spent with Lucan.

She entered the pagoda, a little garden house with seats in it, and by the light of the moon saw water-lotuses glimmering like tiny dancers on the surface of a fishpond. She sat

91

down, a pensive, waiting figure. For what she waited she hardly knew, but it was peaceful here, with the fish stirring the water of their pond and the white flowers moving in a ghostly ballet.

When she heard footfalls this time, her heart jumped and brought her to her feet. A tall figure loomed in the doorway of the pagoda, shutting out the moonlight.

'It is you, Kara?'

'Yes, Lucan.' Her voice was lost and his name came out in a whisper.

'What's the matter?' He stepped inside and the peaked roof seemed to come lower and the woven walls to close in about the two of them. 'I found your mask on one of the paths—is the masquerade over for you?'

'Yes,' she said again. 'Yes, Lucan, it's over, and I am going away from the Isle de Luc this time.'

'You sound strange—as though something has upset you.' His eyes gleamed down at her through the slits of his mask. 'Was it all that carnival nonsense in the pavilion? Surely you can take a bit of fun?'

'Of course I can.' She spoke wearily, fed up with people treating her as an adolescent and either making threats, or scoffing. 'I—I'm tired—today has been a long, noisy one and I think I would like to go back to the hotel. I can go alone—'

'First you will tell me what is wrong.' His hand shot out and gripped her wrist. 'As I came looking for you, I passed the woman who spoke to you at the hotel. There was something about her—a look of breathless pleasure, as though she had just slapped someone, or been kissed. I would say from the look of her that she would get a lot of pleasure out of slapping someone, and she would not need her hand to do it. Tell me, Kara! Has that woman said something to upset you?'

'It is my business—' Her hand struggled in his and in an instant he captured her other hand and made a prisoner of her. She gazed up at him, wildly . . . alone in the night with a masked devil of a man. . . .

'You will tell me if I have to keep you here all night,' he said grimly. 'The two of us alone in a garden house for the night should really give the gossips a meaty bone to chew on.'

'You would not dare, Lucan!'

'Challenging me?'

The word was like a goad, driving Kara to the limit of her resistance. 'That woman knows my brother,' she said raggedly, 'and she is going to write to tell him that his young sister—whom he happens to love and

93

respect—is having an affair with the notorious Lucan Savidge of Dragon Bay.'

There was a taut moment of silence, and then Lucan let out his breath savagely. 'It seems that I have only to look at a girl,' he muttered. 'Well, let them say such things about my wife and there will be hell to pay!'

Kara went taut, her every nerve shocked wide awake by what he said, then pain gripped her that not once had he mentioned another girl—a girl he meant to marry. Not a whisper about her as they toured Fort Fernand, swam in its green waters and lazed on the sands. Not a hint when he persuaded Kara to keep him company until he went home to Dragon Bay.

'Congratulations,' she said in a brittle voice. 'If you had let me know before, I would have bought the bride a present.'

'Would you?' He gave a mocking laugh. 'Do brides usually buy themselves a wedding gift?'

Kara stared up at him, and her heart beat so hard that it made her feel weak. 'Lucan, what are you saying? I—I don't understand you.'

'I am proposing to you,' he said quizzically. 'I want you to be my wife.'

'No—!' She tried to pull away from him.

'You don't have to offer to marry me because of that hateful woman and her threats. I would rather die—'

'Thanks!' His hands felt as though they could have crushed her. 'Of all the answers a man expects when he proposes, that is about the least flattering. Am I so unattractive, Kara?'

'You are a man who could have any woman. Many would be only too flattered,' Kara said quietly. 'I prefer to be loved.'

'You want me to say I love you?' he asked.

'No.' Her eyes raised to his face were blind with the moonlight. 'But I would like to ask why a man who snaps his fingers at convention should suddenly turn conventional. Why, Lucan, do you ask me to be your wife?'

'Because I need a wife,' he said simply. 'A girl with courage and spirit enough to come with me to Dragon Bay. To live in the Great House, with the sound of the waves crashing on to the beach at night, and rich scents rising from the cocoa valley during the day. Would it not compensate, Kara?'

'For what?' she asked. 'What do I give in return?'

'Yourself.' And then, more shattering than anything else, his hands shaped a heart and fitted her face into them. 'It is quite simple.

My brother can no longer provide the heir to the House of Savidge. For generations the Savidges have lived at Dragon Bay and the line has gone on and on. Now it rests with me to provide the next link in the chain.'

'Then this marriage would be a real one—not in the sense that you love me, but that you would expect to make love to me?' Her heart was shaking as she spoke. 'Lucan, why ask this of me?'

'I ask, but you can of course refuse.' He spoke whimsically. 'You take me, or you leave me. It's as simple and as final as that.'

His hands drew away from her face and he pulled off his mask and put his head to show himself unmasked in the moonlight. There was a magnificent insolence about the action. He was straight out of Shelley, Kara thought, full of a pagan pride that said: 'I am what I am, and cannot pretend to be otherwise.'

Kara looked at him and thought of her brother Paul, who was also a man in every sense of the word, defiant and proud, and capable of great suffering in silence. The chirring of cicadas was loud in the silence of this profound moment, one that could change her life for better or worse.

'Come, don't the Greeks say that reflection produces timidity?' Even as Lucan spoke,

96

there was a sound of bursting fireworks and a cascade of stars seemed to fill the sky for a moment. Kara ran out of the pagoda to watch the display, and Lucan strode after her. He caught hold of her shoulders and held her back from further flight. Held her in bondage to feelings she had never dreamed of—so unlike her feeling for Nikos. In that there had been liking and laughter—in this Lucan stood like a beacon around which she flew like a lost bird.

His hands tightened about her shoulders as a flight of rockets exploded into a thousand pieces of stardust. 'I leave for Dragon Bay in a few days,' he said. 'We would have time to be married, in church if you wished.'

'Yes,' the word seemed to pass her lips of its own accord. 'I would like to be married in a church, if that is possible, Lucan.'

* * *

On Monday morning he took her to a little side-street shop with windows that jutted and distorted the shape of the antiques on display. The scent bottles and snuff-boxes; the old clocks and figurines. And there in the musky interior of the shop he bought her a gold wedding-ring with a pattern of tiny lilies carved

97

round it, and an engagement ring set with a large flawless pearl. He slipped the pearl ring on to her finger, looking serious as he admired the effect.

'I could not have wished for anything lovelier, Lucan,' she said, and it did not occur to her at the time that the pearl was like a glimmering teardrop on her hand.

They hurried in opposite directions after they came out of the jeweller's, he to buy a special licence, Kara to send off a wire to her brother and his wife. They must be told that she was getting married, but she shrank inwardly from Paul's reaction to her news. As head of a Greek household he expected to meet and approve the man she wished to marry. She knew that he had always hoped to give her away himself, and to Nikos, and when he received her wire he would probably assume that she was marrying Lucan Savidge on the rebound.

Her heart held misgivings as she came out of the post office. Was it on the rebound from Nikos that she was marrying Lucan? Had she really given enough serious thought to what life at Dragon Bay would be like, in that big, isolated house where Lucan's crippled brother was the master?

She glanced at her left hand, and it was

then that the pearl took on the semblance of a large teardrop and made her think of the old superstition about pearls. They were said to bring tears!

Thrusting this thought from her mind, she went in search of a smart dress shop, where she bought an attractive little dress with a cowl neckline, and a tiny hat made of white velvet flowers with bead centres. She bought white gloves, and then gave her name and hotel to the *vendeuse* so the boxes could be delivered.

'Almost the outfit of a bride,' gushed the *vendeuse*. 'Is *mademoiselle* to be married?'

When Kara nodded, a gleam lit the woman's eyes. 'Perhaps I know the gentleman,' she said inquisitively. 'I am sure I saw *mademoiselle* at the carnival with Monsieur Savidge—'

'You did,' Kara said drily. 'We are to be married on Wednesday.' And as she made her way out of the shop, the *vendeuse* was hurrying to break the news to one of her colleagues.

'Some of the more curious are bound to be at the church to see us married,' Lucan said, when they met for lunch at their favourite harbour restaurant. 'The notorious Lucan Savidge will be making an honest woman of you, my love.'

My love, she thought, her gaze upon him over the rim of her coffee cup. If only he said it without that smile of cynicism!

'A church is a cold place without people in it,' she said. 'I am glad there will be people at our wedding, even if they only come out of curiosity.'

His eyes flicked her grave face, and tousled hair. 'You hardly look old enough to be a bride, Kara. At home on your Greek island, I imagine you would have been married very properly in white silk and yards of family lace.'

'And Paul would have given me away,' she sighed.

'I am sorry there will be no lace, no family—and no young Greek at your side.'

'I am only sorry that Paul and Domini will not be with me,' she said, flushing. 'What of your own family, Lucan? Won't they be surprised when you arrive home with a bride?'

'Not really,' he said. 'Pryde expects me to marry, and my sister Clare has little or no interest in anything but her sculpture. Rue, of course, will be disappointed that she was not at the wedding. The child likes a little gaiety, and there is little enough of that at Dragon Bay.'

Kara slowly put down her coffee cup and

gazed wide-eyed at her husband-to-be. 'Well,' she said, 'you might have told me before that you had a sister who sculpts—and who is this child Rue?'

'Rue?' He tinkered with a spoon. 'She is eight years old and she lives with us at Dragon Bay. She was left on our doorstep—a mere baby in a basket, whose mother had abandoned her. Pryde adopted her. If she had been a boy—'

There he broke off, his eyebrows drawn together in almost a frown as he beckoned their waiter and asked for his bill. They went out into the sunshine and turned their steps in the direction of the hilltop church that reared its turrets into the tropical blue sky. Kara walked silently at Lucan's side. Her heart was beating unevenly. If the child whom Pryde had adopted had been a boy, there would have been no need for Lucan to be taking as wife a girl he hardly knew—and did not love.

Kara stopped walking and she was tugging at the pearl ring on her finger as she said agitatedly: 'I can't go through with it, Lucan. You will have to find someone else to—'

'That ring stays where it is!' He caught hold of her left hand and forcibly pushed the ring back into place. His face was utterly ruthless in that moment; his eyes the colour of

101

a stormy sea, his mouth hard, and his jaw set. 'You promised to marry me, Kara, and by Lucifer you are going to stand by that promise!'

Her hand was held firmly in his as he marched her along the path of the church to a side door. Half an hour later Kara came out dazed into the hot sunshine, her marriage to Lucan all arranged and due to take place on Wednesday morning.

As they went down the path, Kara saw a butterfly clinging to a flower, beating its wings as if held fast to the pollen on the petals of the fiery hibiscus. Kara's heart beat like those wings; she wanted to fly away from what held her. To fly, and yet to stay and be lost as the butterfly was suddenly lost in the heart of the bell flower.

'When next we walk down this path,' said Lucan, 'we will be husband and wife.'

The sun caught the pearl of her ring and it gleamed with captive colours as he swung her hand and looked at her with a curious smile in his sea-coloured eyes.

'I believe the bride-price equalled four cows in the days of Niall the Pirate,' she said with forced lightness.

He put back his head and laughed, his hair showing glints of fire in the blaze of the sun.

'Is that how you see yourself, my girl, the booty of an Irish pirate? You will get along famously with Rue. She delights in the fact that the Savidges trace their beginnings to the warriors of Ulster, and that the grand staircase of the Great House was wrought from the Spanish wood of a wrecked corsair galleon.'

'Rue is a wry name to give a child,' said Kara.

'The mother was no doubt rueful,' he said drily. 'We like to regard the other meaning of the word—herb of grace. She is very graceful, and full of mischief.'

'I—look forward to meeting her, Lucan. To tell you the truth—'

'You are relieved there will be a child in the house.' For a moment his fingers tightened painfully on hers, and she was reminded vividly of what he had said at the moment of his proposal—that his main reason for marrying was to provide an heir for the Great House.

Her heart quickened. In so short a time this tall, savagely attractive man would be her husband . . . her lover. . . .

★   ★   ★

Kara awoke to the dawn rapture of the

birds of the island—today she became the bride of Lucan Savidge.

The next few hours passed all too swiftly. She ate breakfast alone, for she and Lucan must not meet until they met in church, and at nine o'clock she began to dress for her wedding. Her hair had been shampooed the day before and was looking like the soft, sleek cap of a young child, and she removed the little gold rings from her ears and replaced them with the tiny pearls Lucan had bought her yesterday to match her ring.

'No,' she had said, when he gave her the little box.

'Yes,' he said. 'The bride-price has gone up this year.'

She faced the mirror and saw her lips curve into a smile as she smoothed the cowl collar of her dress. The white cowl made her look almost like a young nun about to take her vows, and her smile was too fleeting to hide her fine-drawn look this morning.

She gave a nervous jump as fingers suddenly tapped upon her door. She went to open it, and there was Nap, beaming all over his face and holding the spray of white and gold rosebuds which Kara had chosen to carry in church. The scent of the flowers filled the room as Kara took them from Nap.

'This come too, *mam'zelle*.' He handed her a small envelope and then stood staring at her as though never before had he seen a bride-to-be.

'Please wait, Nap.' She withdrew into her room and set aside her bouquet so she could open the wire. Her fingers shook, her throat went dry, and a cloud passed over the morning. Paul forbade her marriage to a man unknown to him, and ordered her to return home to Andelos!

He did not send his love, and that on top of his anger and disapproval brought quick tears to her eyes. She blinked them away determinedly, for it would bring bad luck for her to weep on her wedding morning. She went to the dressing-table where her handbag lay and rummaged in it for her pen and notebook. She tore out a page and wrote on it, shakily:

'*Dear Paul, when you receive this I shall be married to Lucan. Please forgive, and understand. My best love, Kara.*'

She folded the piece of notepaper and handed it to Nap with some money and instructions to send it off at once for her. A tear had splashed on to the paper, and her voice shook. She strove for calmness and picked up her bouquet and buried her face in the cool,

105

ferny roses. White roses for innocence, golden for warmth.

At a quarter to ten, Kara was ready and Nap was at her door to tell her the hired car awaited her at the side entrance of the hotel. Her hotel bill had been paid the evening before and she did not linger here any longer. Nap followed her down the patio stairs with her suitcases and put them in the car for her. She was aware of people watching her from the balcony above, curious and silent.

'Come with me to the church, Nap,' she said on impulse, and he climbed into the car and sat beside her, surely the most picturesque pageboy that ever attended a bride.

He chattered all the way to the hilltop church. Kara clutched her spray of rosebuds and felt curiously numb.

It was like that all through the wedding ceremony. As if in a dream she stood beside Lucan in the church, with its sprinkling of people in the pews, its coral pillars and baroque panelling, the sunlight turned to jewel colours by the stained glass windows.

Flowers were massed at either side of the altar, great clusters of tropical blooms. Kara guessed that Lucan had arranged to have them put there and she glanced at him in shy gratitude. He was very erect and tall at her side in his tropic worsted, his tie superbly knotted against his white shirt, a small golden rose in his buttonhole. Her heart misgave her when his eyes met hers, then a smile warmed their sea-green depths and she felt less lonely and unsure of him.

CHAPTER FOUR

THE river on which they travelled by raft pursued its course through wild and lovely country. Birds suddenly disturbed fluttered like living jewels against the green walls of the forest, where mossy lianas hung like snakes and big jungle flowers grew in abundance, tongued and alive as great spiders.

Every now and then they shot the shining curve of a waterfall on the long, graceful raft that was made from plantain-logs and bamboo. Their Carib punter stood at the narrow end, looking like a jungle warrior with his high-boned face and tilting eyes beneath a black fringe of hair. The blade of his paddle was studded with shells and scraps of coloured glass and it glittered as it rose and fell. He was lean and copper-coloured, outlined by the sun like a carved idol.

'They were cannibals once,' Lucan said from his seat that faced Kara's. He smiled at the shocked widening of her eyes, and flicked ash from his cheroot into the water. 'Their mode of courtship is intriguing. When a girl "fills the eye" of one of them, he invites her into the high woods and there he *takes* her, you understand, like a warrior. Afterwards she is his woman and they marry.'

The Carib began to chant a song of his ancient race, and it blended with the wild country into which Kara was being swept with every stroke of the great, decorated paddle.

'He sings a wedding chant in our honour.' Lucan sat back lazily in his low wicker seat and stretched his long legs. The white silk of his shirt clung to the muscles of his chest and shoulders, his throat showed hard and brown in the opening of his collar, from which he had stripped his tie. The silvery green river light was in his eyes.

'Do you still feel a stranger to yourself, Mrs. Savidge?' he drawled.

She nodded, and then said lightly: 'Change the name but not the letter, change for worse instead of better.'

'Do you expect life with me to be—worse?' His eyes narrowed to a glittering green. 'I am not a boy, Kara, to kneel before you and make promises of heaven, but life with me here on earth will not be dull, I promise you. I work hard, and I want someone to come home to when the sun sets red across the cane fields.'

Someone . . . anyone. Kara glanced away from him at the wild cane brakes they were passing. She saw great white birds in the rushes, and women from the isolated houses doing the family wash at the riverside, using boulders on which to bleach their cottons in the sun.

'When will we reach Dragon Bay?' she asked.

'Some time tomorrow morning.' He tossed the butt of his cheroot into the water and it floated away beneath a great elephant's ear. 'We will not travel through the night as I usually do—the river grows treacherous as it nears the sea—but will make camp in the forest just before sundown.'

Her heart raced—so her bridal night was to be spent among those giant trees and shiny green shield-plants that might be hiding warriors in ambush!

'I am longing for my first glimpse of the Great House,' she said, a tiny nervous shake in her voice. 'Have you wired your family, Lucan? Do they know you are bringing home a—bride?'

'No,' he said lazily. 'I thought we would give them a surprise.'

'Lucan—' She was disconcerted, and did not look forward to being an unexpected, even unwelcome surprise. 'I think it might have been more tactful of you to let them know. Your sister might not like adjusting her household arrangements at the last moment.'

'Clare?' He put back his head and laughed. 'She doesn't bother with the running of the house—that is left to Da, who used to be in charge of the nursery when we were children. Clare is not the domesticated type. She lives only for her art,' he added mockingly.

'I see.' Kara dabbled her fingers in the water and didn't know how pensive her profile was. 'What will your family think of me, I wonder?'

He gazed at the strained triangle that was her face, and the spray-wet hair that clung to her slim young neck and thin cheeks. A smile came fleetingly to her sensitive mouth as she met his eyes; from nervousness she went to shyness, and then to confusion as his green gaze slipped to her lips. The spray over the bows of the raft had stung them berry-red.

'You have a certain wild Greek charm,' he drawled. 'You will have to use it to slay the dragon.'

'The dragon?' she whispered.

'Pryde, my brother. He is my twin, remember, and he cannot leap on a horse and ride out the devils that pursue all the Savidges.'

She drew a shaky breath. 'I begin to be

afraid, Lucan. You said that it takes the strong and the ruthless to live at Dragon Bay. Will I be strong enough?'

'Surely it took courage and daring to marry me, Kara?' His look was one of irony, as though no woman could have tender reasons for marrying him. 'By the way, did you receive an answer to the wire you sent to your brother?'

She nodded, and felt a sinking at heart.

'Tell me what he had to say.'

'Oh, the usual—'

'The exact words, Kara!'

'All right.' She flung up her head almost defiantly. 'He forbade my marriage to a man unknown to him and ordered me to return home to Andelos.'

Silence and shadow fell down about them as they entered one of the cool tree tunnels where the river narrowed and the raft almost touched the banks at either side. Leaves shifted and dappled Lucan's face, and then they were out again into the sunshine and shooting a series of miniature rapids with aplomb, the spray like a soft rain that made Kara blink rapidly.

'Paul would have wired in that way n-no matter who I chose to marry,' she said.

'But not if it had been the estimable Nikos.'

Lucan gave his sardonic laugh and caught hold of her left hand. He studied the gold band upon it, and the pearl that glimmered like a teardrop. 'He probably thinks that you have married me on the rebound—have you, I wonder?'

He released her hand, and the next moment was on his feet and walking across the raft with a catlike precision. He stood beside the Carib punter and Kara could hear them talking together in the Carib dialect.

Lucan's white shirt and smooth beige trousers emphasized the strong, active lines of him. His foxfire hair was tousled by the flying spray. Her husband, and yet so dangerously unknown, who aroused in her a feeling that mingled with fear like a sweet wine with a bitter one, until the two were a blend that intoxicated.

Mon coeur diable, she thought. My heart's devil.

Suddenly, as she watched him, the Carib pointed into the underbrush of the left bank of the river, towards which he had steered in order to avoid a large floating tree. He said something in an excited tone of voice and Lucan immediately took the paddle, then to Kara's amazement the Carib leapt ashore and disappeared among the crowding ferns and vine-veiled trees.

'Is anything wrong?' she asked.

'Far from it.' Lucan flashed her a smile, and the paddle dripped as he rested it and held the raft steady. 'He set a pig trap on the way upriver and, with luck, we will celebrate our wedding with a feast.'

All was still in the forest, and then Kara tensed in her seat as a sudden loud squeal broke the silence. 'Our dinner,' she said, feeling a pang for the victim.

'Our wedding supper,' Lucan drawled.

The Carib returned in triumph with a small black pig, his knife again in its sheath at his hip. Lucan clapped him on the shoulder, and a minute later the raft was skimming along and Kara's husband and the savage-looking Carib were chanting a song which sounded as old and elemental as the forest all around.

*　　*　　*

Purple shadows were adrift in the forest as their raft crossed the dazzling bar of the setting sun. The man who steered this unusual craft seemed a figure cast in bronze, and Kara felt the turning of her heart as they headed for a sandy bay where mangroves stood like

114

giants in the gathering dusk.

'This is Frenchman's Bay,' said Lucan, 'where long ago a notorious pirate sloop used to hide out. The captain made off with an ancestress of mine, but from all accounts he was quite a charmer and she was quite rattled when rescued by the French Navy.'

Lucan's eyes were full of diablerie as they met Kara's, and she watched as he leapt to the beach and secured the mooring-rope of the raft to a firm boulder.

They were busily making camp when the sun burst into flame and spilled its last embers on to the river. A violet stillness followed, and then came darkness, and a bird broke plaintively into song and out of it.

Kara spread the bright Carib rugs near the barbecue-fire which Lucan was carefully building. Their punter, Julius, was cleaning the pig, and soon it was spitted and set to barbecue, while knobbly yams were set to bake at the edges of the fire.

'This is an ideal place to make camp,' said Lucan. 'It's one of nature's larders—come, I'll show you.'

She followed him in among the trees and was aware at once of their aloneness in the forest, musky with wild flower scents and the sap of the entangling vines. He switched on the torch which he had brought off the raft and directed its beam along the trunks of the trees. Something scampered, and then in the shifting light Kara saw clusters of fruit sheltering beneath large circular leaves.

'Paw-paws.' Lucan handed her the torch and while she held it steady he reached up and plucked some of the patchy-gold globes that hung above his tall head.

Quite soon Kara's conical straw hat was bulging with the tropical fruits that grew wild and abundant in the forest, and they began to make their way back to camp, surrounded by a chorus of frog croaks and whistles and the persistent chirring of cicadas.

It was all new and exciting to Kara; a mysterious world of shadows and sounds that would have been unnerving if Lucan had not been with her. Once he was very close as he disentangled her from a clinging vine, and at the touch of his fingers she shivered and her heartbeats quickened. Tonight she would lie in his arms beneath the stars of this wild land and be made truly part of the Savidge tradition.

The tradition, the pride, and the obligation that had forced Lucan into marriage.

'What are you thinking?' he asked suddenly.

She almost told him, for here it was intimately dim with the torchlight a gold pool at their feet. She almost said that if he did not want her heart's love, then it would have been kinder of him to let her go.

'I would enjoy a bathe in the river,' she said. 'The water glimmers so invitingly.'

'Yes, it does look cool and inviting.' He followed her glance to the river through the trees.

'May I have a dip in it, Lucan?'

'Of course.' He gave a laugh and feathered her cheek with his thumb. 'You are being a submissive bride.'

'I merely wondered if the water was safe to bathe in.'

'Much safer than a plunge into matrimony with a Savidge,' he mocked. 'Supper will not be ready yet, so I think I will join you.'

Kara changed into her bathing suit beneath the leafy tent of a rainfall tree at the river's edge, her senses thrilling to the cool, dark caress of the water as she slipped into it. How often she and Nikos had swam in the wine-dark waters of Andelos at night, laughing and carefree, not thinking of tomorrow or questioning the future.

She heard behind her what sounded like a water-plopper in the shallows, and she grabbed handfuls of reflected stars as she swam and breathed the lush night air, spiced with the forest scents all around.

What strange surprises life held! Even yet she could not take in the reality of all this, and she gave herself a pinch and laughed at her own foolishness. The river, the stars, the forest were real enough—

So, too, the masculine arms that were suddenly around her in the water. She fought them instinctively, and heard Lucan laugh. 'What a nervous bride!' His teeth flashed in the starlight, and though he let her slip away, to seemingly escape, he came after her again, and this time she felt less playfulness in him as he took hold of her, less fight in herself. She was helpless in his arms as he carried her up the opposite bank of the river to the shadowed sands. There he laid her down and she felt his hands on her shoulders, and then his face pressed against her.

'Don't let us think about tomorrow—and Dragon Bay.' It was a groan, crushed against her temple by his lips. 'Let's forget everything—let's pretend that I married you for my sake only.'

His lips burned their warmth into her throat, his lips smudged from hers a hurt protest. Her slim body was pressed close to the hard beat of his heart, to the warm strength of his body—but she had gone cold to her heart. He had married her for Pryde's sake . . . he had to pretend it was for his own!

With a supreme effort she turned her face from his searching lips. 'Yes, let us be honest with each other, Lucan.' She dragged the words out of the heart that bled from his honesty. 'I married you because my pride could not bear pity from those who thought Nikos wanted me. There, now we start even! You married me for Pryde's sake—I married too for pride's sake.'

The silence that fell between them was filled with the chirring of the cicadas. She felt heartbeats her heart could have counted, then Lucan released her and stood up. He towered over her, his face dark, his hands clenched at his sides, then he turned and splashed into the river, leaving silvery trails in his wake as he swam away in the direction of the campfire, where sparks leapt up about the feast pig on its spit.

'*Chairete*,' Kara thought, as she rose out of the sands where Lucan had held her as if to love her. She would not have asked for words of tenderness, but there had been words in his heart and he had spoken them—words that made their marriage a cage, which he had entered with a snarl in his heart.

'*Chairete*,' she sighed, as she walked down tiredly to the river's edge. 'Rejoice in this your marriage, Kara. Go share your wedding supper with your bridegroom. Share his food and wine; share his home but not his heart.'

*   *   *

The barbecued pig was meltingly tender, crackling and juicy and spiced with forest herbs their Carib had hunted out with his keen nose. The yams tasted delicious baked on an open fire with their skins burnt to charcoal.

Kara had not eaten very much all day and now she ate with automatic appetite, using her fingers to hold her pork chop, and too elemental at heart not to love all this—the smoky tang of the meat, the sparks like firebeetles in the air—with that mixture of gaiety and sadness which is so very Greek.

She glanced across at her husband in the firelight, free to watch him because he was listening to the song their Carib was singing. Julius had a deep, natural voice and none of the inhibitions of the civilized. He sang because he liked to, and because Lucan his master enjoyed his songs. Old as time, their source lost in the history of the Caribbean.

Kara studied the creases either side of Lucan's mouth, the gleam of his eyes, and his hair that was like dark fire. Fate had led her over the threshold of his room at the Hotel Victoire, and tomorrow she must cross with him the threshold of the Great House. Not in his arms as a beloved bride—of that she could be unbearably sure—but as the companion of his strange fate.

It was then that Kara became aware of a strange animal crouching some distance from the fire, but close enough for the glitter of its eyes to be seen, and its dragon-like shape.

She watched it tensely, unaware that the Carib song had come to an end until Lucan spoke. 'Don't be nervous,' he said. 'The iguana—the little dragon—is quite harmless.'

'Make bamboo chicken breakfast,' chortled Julius, but Lucan shook his head.

'Let the fellow be,' he said. 'He reminds me of the bronze dragon on our mantel at the house.'

And then, with a ponderous shuffle, the iguana made off into the forest and Kara was left with the odd feeling that he had been a sign, a warning that the Savidge dragon was a threat to the Savidge brides. She gave a shiver and Lucan must have noticed. He poured her another mug of coffee and handed it across to her. 'Thank you.' She held the mug in both hands and sipped gratefully at the hot, sweet contents.

'Wait till you taste our Dragon Bay chocolate.' Lucan opened his knife and began to rip the carapace of a green avocado. 'We add cinnamon, as the Incas used to, and then a thick dob of cream. I love it. I always have, right from a boy.'

And then his face hardened, as if mention of his boyhood brought him memories less sweet. Memories of the mother who, Kara suspected, had doted on Pryde but not on Lucan. The younger twin who may have given her a difficult and painful time at his birth; a wide-shouldered, restless boy with a passionate temper. He had mentioned his mother only twice to Kara, once to say that she had been French, the second time to point out cynically that he was scarred on the cheek from a lash of her riding whip.

He dug the stones out of the centre of the avocado and tossed them into the fire. Then he speared a piece of the pale green fruit on the point of his knife and held it out to Kara. She took it and wished that she and Lucan could spend all their tomorrows, all their

122

nights, alone like this, forgetful of the world and its obligations.

Julius sat smoking a strong cigar, and when it was finished he got to his feet and picked up his Carib rug. 'Goodnight, Masser Lucan. Goodnight, mistress,' he said, and he retired to the raft to sleep, leaving them alone by the fire.

Alone, whispered the leaves. Alone, chirred the cicadas.

'It was a good supper,' Kara murmured.

'We have not yet opened our bottle of wine,' he said.

'No—' She gazed beyond the fire and saw winged foxes like flying shadows among the trees.

'We should drink a toast to our bridal.' There was a note of irony in his voice, and Kara gave a jump as the cork popped and the wine glowed red as blood as Lucan poured it out into their empty coffee mugs. 'We never seem to have any wine glasses,' he drawled. 'Here you are, Mrs. Savidge. You had wine and a song even if there were no lanterns to light the feast.'

'*Chairete*.' She drank her wine in quick sips, and her eyes grew wide until they were full of Lucan as he rose to his feet and stepped over to her. Their eyes clung as he knelt and pressed her back on the Carib rug. He took the mug from her hand, and then calmly tucked the end of the rug over her feet and cocooned her in its folds. He lifted her head and tucked beneath it his rolled-up jacket, to which clung cheroot smoke and the lingering scent of the rose still in the buttonhole.

'Go to sleep,' he said. 'We start early for Dragon Bay.'

'Lucan—'

'Go to sleep,' he cut in. 'Dream of the boy-lover who never bruised you with a kiss, but who knew how to break your heart.'

'Oh, Lucan—'

'My dear,' the fire played its shadows over his saturnine face, 'the Wagnerian sword will not always share our bed, I promise you, but you have had a long, tiring day, and tomorrow will be full of new events for you to cope with. Are you warm?'

'As a little cat,' she said huskily.

'Then goodnight.' He bent briefly and kissed her. The smoke of the fire clung to his ruffled hair—the bitter-sweetness of the wine to his lips. And soon she slept, her cheek pressed against the golden rosebud he had worn to their wedding.

CHAPTER FIVE

THEY breakfasted on fish caught at the river's edge, and began the second half of their journey as dawn splintered the sky with colour, beautiful and flamy. A mist hung over the river, fine as gold tulle, and the whistle of a solitaire floated across, clear and promising to Kara's ears.

So much verdure and richness, woods that rose high and bird haunted and fell suddenly into giant punch-bowls. Kara drank it all in with her big Greek eyes, while the river unwound like a silk ribbon and drew them onward to the Bay of the Dragon.

'It is all so different from Greece,' she said to Lucan. 'There we have a barren grandeur, a soil that gives with reluctance, but here everything is so green.'

She met his eyes, green as the leaves on the trees that stood like giants to watch the raft go skimming by. She recalled her awakening at the camp-site and how it had disturbed her to see him half in, half out of the folds of his Carib rug, still fast asleep, his face relaxed into a ghost of the boyishness he had long since left behind him.

Right now, long legs straddled to take the motion of the raft beneath him, he looked a stranger to all tenderness. The sun capped his hair like a helmet of bronze; each impulse and muscle of his lean body was trained and conditioned to meet challenge.

Could marriage with such a man ever be secure and warmly intimate, as marriage should be? A haven for a woman, in which she could be released from the fears and inhibitions that raged in her until she was truly loved. Kara gazed at Lucan and knew in her heart that they could never be close because too much held them apart—foremost his obligation to Pryde. It ruled all his actions. It was the impulse that had led him into marriage—when the impulse should be love—and when they had a son he would be given to the Great House so that the Savidge tradition could continue, ever onward like this river.

Fast-flowing now, and widening as it began to merge with the sea. Rocks began to appear, and the masses of verdure on their left began to fall away until when Kara glanced behind her the mass of greenery was lost in the silvery green of the sea.

As the colour of the water changed, so did Lucan's eyes. They were glittering, and Kara knew by their look of expectation—and re-bellion—that the raft drew nearer all the time to Dragon Bay.

'We are running with the currents beyond the bay,' he said to her. 'Hold tight to the arms of your seat, for this part of the trip is the roughest.'

And so it proved, the raft pitching like driftwood on the turbulent waters of the bay as Julius steered it between a forked tongue of rocks towards a more placid lagoon, sparkling in the sun like a pot of melted emeralds. Sheer above the lagoon, its lower terraces of stone licked at by the sea, was the House of the Dragon. Remote-looking, a stronghold that had held centuries of Savidges, its atmosphere even from here one of mystery and brooding.

Kara caught her breath in awe, for the house was so massive, built to defy all the elements and all its enemies, its windows flashing like eyes, and its wings spread to receive the new bride, the stranger.

'Castles are proud things, but it's safest to be outside them.' That line of Emerson's leapt into her mind as spray leapt the sides of the raft and flew in her eyes and clung like rain-drops to her dark hair. Blinking her lashes to clear them of spray, she saw Lucan devouring the house with his eyes, his sardonic mask stripped away, a look on his face of tortured love and hate. Kara glanced quickly away as something twisted into her heart, a barb of sheer jealousy, lunatic jealousy, for a house was just a mass of stone, mortar and tile, not a human being that could feel, and love.

The stab of pain left its hurt as Julius steered the raft to the landing-stage of the lagoon. He leapt up to secure the mooring-rope, and Kara felt the encirclement of Lucan's arms—steel that rippled—as he swung her up off the raft on to the stone quay.

Coral-trees waved their tresses on the strip of beach, and sea-flowers clung to the water-level terraces of the house. They were like giant steps, those terraces, carved from the stone of the cliffs and dropping one after the other into the green water.

'We call it the Dragon's Stairway,' said Lucan. He scanned her, from her spray-wet hair to her sandalled feet, and once again he swept her up in his arms, the water swirling about his ankles as he mounted the first of the terraces. She rested tensely against his hard shoulder, until upon the fourth step he lowered her to her feet.

'There is another way up to the house,' he pointed along the beach to where the cliffs rounded a bend. 'Engineers tunnelled out the rock in my grandfather's time and put in a lift—rather like a miner's cage—absolutely safe, but it doesn't provide the romantic view that we get from these terraces.'

She saw Julius carrying their suitcases along the beach. When he reached the bend he turned to flash them a smile; a descendant of a fierce tribe, his skin the colour of strong rum, his devotion to Lucan that of a friend rather than a servant. The Irish blood in Lucan could not tolerate servitude, his rebel spirit could not abide bondage ... Kara, his bride, was the only creature in bondage to Lucan Savidge.

Side by side they climbed the Dragon's Stairway, and the boom of the sea followed them, arching into glittering combers that built into silver palaces and then crashed and tumbled. Green lizards—like miniature dragons—basked and panted in the sun, and then flowers began to spill upon the terraces and Kara touched with beauty-greedy hands the petals of vivid cannas, the golden trumpets on sprawling vines, and the lips of snapdragons.

A pair of magnificent immortelles made an archway of orange and yellow blossoms, and Kara passed beneath them, followed by Lucan, her small cry of wonder like that of a bird when it takes its first flight into the unknown.

The Great House—fire-gold in the sun, set high by the pride and arrogance of the Savidge rebels who had first set their mark on this land that yielded the white gold of sugar, the dark lush cocoa, and the spices that travelled to all the tables of the world.

A flight of halfmoon steps led to the portico, where above the massive front door the Dragon crest was cut deep in the stone, with beneath it the Savidge motto.

The columns of the portico had dragons carved round their bases, and columned piazzas spread like wings along the sides of the house, ending in stone follies, temple-like, hung with masses of bougainvillea. The blossoms were alive in the sun, like flame running riot, and above were the storeys that held innumerable rooms, galleried and door-windowed.

'From the rear of the house we overlook the cocoa valley,' Lucan was looking intent as he fired a cheroot. 'The left wing overlooks the sea, the right wing the cane fields. We dominate our possessions, Kara, lords of all we survey . . . Pryde's the heritage, mine the allegiance.'

'It's awesome,' she said breathlessly.

'You will get used to it. Come, we will go in this way.' He piloted her to the right and up the flight of steps in the centre of the piazza. Door-windows faced them, which he opened with a hint of a flourish, and Kara stepped into the immense hall of the Great House.

She walked across the parquet floor as though treading on cat-ice, for it was so forbidding, so grand, not a home but a house made for giants. Lustrous island timbers had been used to panel the walls, heavy silver stood upon great sideboards, and crested mirrors reflected the rosewood and mahogany, the tall winged chairs, and silvery Waterford chandeliers, agleam with crystal drops that stirred and tinkled in the whirring of antique fans.

Kara saw the dragon of bronze on the mantel of the great fireplace, and the big golden goblet that was older than this house, the cup which the lusty Savidges had pledged to buy land and which they had redeemed as they began to make their fortune.

'This is all so—palatial, Lucan.' She gazed around her as though lost. 'I—I had no idea you were such a rich family.'

He gave a laugh as he flicked ash into the fireplace. 'The days when the Savidges could afford Waterford crystal and paintings by the

Masters are over, Kara. We derive a fair income from the plantations, but gone are the days when Sugar was a monarch and fortunes were amassed by men like my ancestor there.'

He gestured at a nearby portrait of a young man in a dark maroon cutaway coat, white ruffled shirt, embossed waistcoat and stock of pale blue silk. A dandy of another century, the deep-set mocking eyes capturing her gaze for a long moment. She turned again to Lucan—but for his modern clothes he might have stepped down out of that massive frame.

'Another Savidge, another time,' he said, the same mocking light in his eyes, 'but the blood does not change.'

And then for the first time Kara asked a question that was often in her mind. 'Are you and your brother identical twins, Lucan?'

He frowned slightly and seemed to be listening for something. 'In a few minutes you will see for yourself the likeness and the difference,' he said enigmatically. He picked up the dragon crested goblet and held it so a ray of sunlight flashed on the gold and the scarlet.

'It is a Savidge custom that a bride and groom pledge themselves to the good of the house by drinking from this cup,' he said. 'This evening we will be expected to make our pledge by sharing the wine that Pryde, as

132

head of the house, will pour into the cup. Will you be willing Kara?'

'I married you to share your life, Lucan,' she said quietly. 'I understand tradition and the tribal feeling—I am a Greek, remember. We also regard the family house as the heart of the family, and I am afraid my brother will take time to forgive me for marrying without his consent.'

'I am sorry about that, Kara.' Lucan reached out and squeezed her cold hand that was not yet used to the weight of his ring, and then she stiffened as a door opened behind her, at the end of the hall. She heard plainly the sound of wheels on the smooth parquet, and then her heart came into her mouth as something huge and black bounded past her and flung up on its haunches to greet Lucan. A mastiff, its heraldic head heavily collared, its great paws on Lucan's shoulders and its eyes glowing with adoration.

'You great fool!' Lucan hugged the beast, and Kara could hear behind her the gradual, deliberate glide of wheels over the floor, nearer, ever nearer, until at last she nerved herself to turn round.

She met eyes so deep-set that she felt lost in them for a frightening moment. She saw a face both handsome and forbidding, with deep lines of pain etched into it, and hair that once had been as fiery as Lucan's but was now streaked with ash-grey. He sat in a wheelchair, yet he made it look like a throne. He made *her* feel the helpless one.

'The news reached me last night, Lucan, that you had married in Fort Fernand.' Pryde's voice was deep and harshly attractive. 'I hope the marriage bell rang merrily for you and Caprice?'

There was a moment of utter silence in the great hall, and then Lucan flung an arm about Kara's shoulders. She wanted to feel grateful, but instead she felt a deadly shrinking of heart and body. Pryde had thought that Lucan was bringing home a bride called Caprice!

'This is Kara.' Lucan said it a shade defiantly. 'We met in Fort Fernand ten days ago, just after I returned from Paris. Kara is Grecian.'

'I see.' Pryde seemed to see into the secret regions of Kara's mind, and the shock it had suffered. Caprice. Who was she? A girl in Paris whom Lucan had hoped to marry?

'Welcome to Dragon Bay, Kara.' A faint smile dispelled the severity of Pryde's expression. 'It is about time a young woman brought the promise of children to this old house. There is Rue, of course, but she needs play-fellows. Has Lucan told you about the child?'

'Yes, *seigneur*.' Kara still felt cold, even within the enclosure of her husband's arm. He might have told her about Caprice and not left her to learn in such a humiliating way that she had a rival. 'I am looking forward to meeting Rue—and Clare.'

'Rue is at her lessons.' He used turn-of-the-century phrases like a man used to living in a world apart. 'Clare is making for herself a man of stone who cannot answer her back, or wound her heart.'

'Clare sounds most sensible.' With a delicacy Kara drew away from Lucan. 'It is not always wise to be a romantic.'

'You are a romantic, of course.' Pryde gestured at the love-seat between the long windows overlooking the piazza, and Kara sat down in the seat. Lucan sprawled in a wing-back chair, the mastiff at his feet, its jowl resting on paws the size of a lion's. Pryde's eyes were brooding, the same diamond-grey as her husband's, with no hint of green in them. The twin brothers looked alike, and yet ten years might have set them apart.

A food trolley was wheeled in by a coloured houseman in a white jacket, and they had coffee where they sat, prawn *vol au vent*, and slices of coffee cake that melted in the mouth.

'I have given you a bridal suite, on the seaward side of the house, Lucan. The Emerald Suite.' Pryde finished his coffee and replaced the cup on the trolley. 'You are fond of the sea, Kara?'

'I was born within sound of it,' she told him. 'I love the churning of the surf, especially at night.'

As she spoke of the night, she flushed slightly at Pryde's quick scrutiny of her face and her person. What was he thinking? That she looked too slim and boyish for the task in hand, that of providing sons for the Great House?

'So until ten days ago you were strangers to each other?' Pryde glanced at his brother, a glitter to his eyes. 'Quite a lightning romance!'

'Quite,' said Lucan, and their glances seemed to cross and clash like foils. 'I think Kara would like to go upstairs now. We spent last night at Frenchman's Bay and slept on the sands. I didn't care to risk the currents of our bay in the dark.'

'Caution, Lucan—you?' Pryde arched an ironical eyebrow. 'Well, as we must discuss the business that took you to Paris, I think it would be advisable for Kara to leave us—business always seems to bore the decorative sex.'

Kara tensed in the love-seat and wondered if Pryde was being a little cruel. He looked as though he could be, for to be made helpless when his vigour had matched Lucan's would be enough to embitter a saint—and no Savidge, she was sure, was ever a saint!

She stood up as a maid came in answer to Pryde's ring. 'You know where to put Mrs. Savidge,' he said. 'I shall not detain your husband too long, Kara. Make yourself at home at Dragon Bay.'

Would such a thing ever be possible? Kara was inclined to doubt it as she went with the maid up the gracious, blackwood staircase. It curved up to gallery after gallery, forming at each curve a perfect horseshoe in which a person might stand to gaze down into the great hall.

On the second gallery, where the maid paused, there was a sudden dance of coloured light from the fable-window which they approached as they walked along the gallery. In the window hovered a girl in a golden dress, who seemed about to float out on to the staircase balcony.

'How unusual,' said Kara, and then she

remembered what Lucan had told her, that the Great House had a ghost who stepped out of a picture window on one of the galleries and walked with a rustle of silk when the house was still and its occupants abed.

A few moments later Kara was alone in the suite she was to share with Lucan. The two bedrooms connected, and what might once have been a large closet for clothes was now a bathroom. There was also a small solarium with ceiling-to-floor windows framing a wonderful view of the waves and rocks of Dragon Bay.

Kara stood gazing down at the bay and she noticed that from here the cliffs were like a towering mass of seashells that gave off a shine as they caught the sun. Were they the cliffs that Lucan and Pryde had attempted to climb long ago? The cliffs from which Pryde had fallen?

Something seemed to tell her they were, and she hastened out of the solarium into her bedroom, striving to wipe from her mind a grim picture of that hurtling figure, and Lucan clinging horrified to the cliff face. Why, she wondered, had Pryde chosen to put his brother and his bride in this particular suite? Because it overlooked the scene of his accident, and he wanted Lucan to remember it each time he glanced out of the window—or took his wife in his arms?

She gazed around her bedroom with pensive eyes. There was a queen-sized fourposter with a frilled canopy of sea-green voile, and carved dragons all the way up its posts almost to the ceiling. A tambour-fronted cabinet stood beside the bed and a French clock stood on it. There were low-backed chairs with silk seats, a satin-wood desk with a nest of drawers, and a vast wardrobe and dressing-table of matching mahogany.

Kara's brush and comb set had been laid out on the dressing-table, and she bit her lip as she studied her reflection in the mirror. No wonder Pryde had stared at her! Her hair was tousled from sea-spray, her nose shiny, and her shirt and trews were hardly bridal.

She had better have a shower and a change of dress. She would put on the pleated white dress that made her look cool and outwardly poised.

She went across to the big wardrobe, where she guessed her dresses had been hung, and she gave a cry of fright as a figure leapt out of the wardrobe and cried, 'Boo!'

'You little wretch!' Kara caught hold of the child. 'That isn't a very funny trick to play on a person. Who are you?'

139

'You did jump,' the child said with glee. She gazed up at Kara with green eyes that danced in a faun's face. Her mane of hair was tawny, streaked with the tints of a ruddy autumn. Her lips were like wild cherries—never had Kara seen a lovelier child!

'Are you Rue?' Kara asked, her flash of temper giving way to interest.

'Yes.' The child smiled—a smile to catch at the heart. 'I am eight years old, and I am sorry I made you jump. Da said you would be spoiled and pretty, and that my nose would be put out of joint because Yunk would not take so much notice of me now he's married. She said all his time would be taken up with keeping his wife happy.'

'And who is Yunk?' Kara asked, fascinated by the recital.

'Lucan, of course.' The child went and sat on the dressing-stool and began to play with Kara's toiletries. 'I call him Yunk because he is my young uncle, don't you see? I have to call him my uncle, but everyone knows that I am really—' There the child broke off and gazed at Kara through the mirror. 'I suppose you are the bride?'

'Yes, I am Lucan's wife.' Kara sat down on the side of her bed and studied this precocious little baggage called Rue. She obviously knew she was adopted, but how very odd that she should have green eyes and hair with reddish tints in it. Any stranger would have taken her for a Savidge!

She lifted the lid off a powder-bowl and dabbed the puff all over her face. 'You don't look very old,' she said, cocking her head to study the effect of the powder.

'I am twenty-one years old,' said Kara with a grin. The child's quaint mode of speech was obviously picked up from Pryde, and the other adults who seemed at Dragon Bay to live in a world that belonged to yesterday. This room must have been like this a hundred years ago; the sound of the sea and the rich smell from the cocoa valley would have wafted in on other brides who came in trepidation to the House of the Dragon.

'Do you think you will like living here with us?' asked Rue, turning on the stool to gaze at Kara with green eyes set in fringes of dark lashes. 'Of course, even if you don't like it here, you will have to stay. Auntie Clare says there is no escape from being a Savidge, and you are a Savidge now.'

Yes, Kara thought, I belong here now, and she tensed on her bed as the bedroom door opened and Lucan came in. His brows were drawn in a frown, but when he saw Rue he broke into a smile. 'Hullo, monkey!' He swung the child off the stool and kissed her. Their russet heads close together gave Kara a shock.

'Did you bring me a present from Paris?' Rue pressed her cheek against his. 'Dear Yunk,' she added.

'Don't I always bring you a present, baggage?' He glanced across at Kara and flicked his eyes over the vast proportions of her bed. 'You look like a frog on a lily-pad, my dear.'

'Charming,' she said, and watched him stride into his bedroom with Rue perched on his shoulder. A couple of minutes later the child came running out. 'Look what I've got!' She wore on her wrist a silver bracelet set with a tiny heart-shaped watch. 'My name is engraved inside the bangle, with special love from Uncle Lucan. I must go and show Da.'

She dashed out of the room, then poked her head round the door. 'I bet Da will be glad to hear that you are not a pampered doll, Kara.'

She scampered away, and Lucan lounged in his bedroom doorway looking amused. 'She's a little devil, eh?'

'Yes,' Kara said thoughtfully. A little devil with her husband's eyes and unruly russet hair. A child who was obviously of the same blood as Lucan!

142

CHAPTER SIX

WHEN the afternoon sun had cooled and the shadows were lengthening, Lucan took Kara on a tour of the plantations. She could ride, and he mounted her on a cream-coloured filly called Silky. His own mount was mettlesome and black as night. Jet the hound went with them, bounding at the hoofs of the stallion.

The sugar cane was planted in endless rows that would, as the weeks went by, grow silver-green and taller than the men who would harvest it by burning off the leaves and cutting down the sugar-loaded cane with sharp cutlasses.

'The fields are already showing their green,' Lucan said, sweeping out an arm and indicating the miles of cane. 'With luck we shall have a good crop this year, and men will come from all parts of the island to harvest the cane and sing the old songs as they swing their cutlasses in the hot sun. It's quite a sight, Kara.'

She could well believe him, and she smiled as she glanced at him. He wore a field hat tilted down over his eyes, such arresting eyes, alight with his pride in the plantations. His horse jibbed as a large-winged creature hopped off a stalk of cane and skimmed the proud head. Lucan soothed his mount with a caressing hand, so brown and work-hardened.

'The cane fields are like a rippling ocean of green,' Kara said, and she did not look beyond this moment to the time of the harvest. They cantered on towards the sugar refinery, with its smoke stacks looking black against the sky. The sun was setting across the fields and the whole scene was grand and unforgettable.

'Would you like to go inside?' Lucan asked.

They dismounted and Kara found that at the present time there was little activity in the big mill. 'The racket is deafening when production is at full gallop,' Lucan said, pointing out the choppers and giant rollers beneath which the cane would be cut small and then crushed, the liquid draining off into huge boilers to be clarified and crystallized.

Kara gazed up at the catwalks above the various tanks and containers and she gave a shiver as she pictured the men at work above the great bubbling cauldrons. The chimneys of the tower would smoke dark into the sun and a hot toffee smell would seep out of the factory as the brown syrup was turned slowly into sugar.

As they rode away they passed a knoll on which stood the ruins of a sugar mill where long ago the grinding had been done by wind-power. The sails now hung limp above the blackened tower, and the late afternoon sun peered through the broken windows. The place had a haunted air, a look of brooding disquiet, and Kara could not resist a backward glance . . . her breath caught in her throat, she could have sworn that someone, something moved in the tower and that for a moment she and Lucan were gazed at through the broken windows.

'Do children play in that old ruin?' she asked.

'I very much doubt it.' Lucan turned to look at her. 'The place is a bit creepy and the coloured folk on the estate steer clear of it—I should like to pull it down, but Pryde likes the bit of mystery that clings to the old mill. It adds colour, he says, for he deplores the modern factories we have to build in order to keep ourselves competitive.'

'Lucan, I am sure I saw someone at that window,' she pointed towards it with her riding-crop.

'It was probably a bat, or your imagination.' His stallion jibbed as he turned in the saddle to take a look at the old mill, with the sun burning red and outlining the bent old sails. A slight wind whispered through the cane and caught at one of the sails, which creaked and then fell silent.

'The place does have an uncanny air.' Then Lucan gave a laugh. 'Perhaps Luella Savidge still waits there for her lover, the young overseer whom she used to meet clandestinely when her husband was away from home.'

'Don't joke, Lucan.' Kara gave a shiver. 'The unhappy dead do leave a kind of atmosphere behind them—'

'Well, we are very much alive, and not unhappy, I hope.' His eyes captured hers. 'What did you think of Pryde?'

'That he is proud, and that he lives in the past—' And then she obeyed a wild impulse and gave her filly a flick of the whip on her silky haunches. With a bound the filly was away into the deepening afternoon light. Jet gave an excited bark, and Kara's heart quickened with a pleasure almost primitive as she heard Lucan's stallion racing after her mount.

Along a corridor through the cane galloped the two riders, the sun swooning in the west as they came to the cocoa valley and reined in above the forest of cocoa trees, the ripe smell of the pods hanging rich in the warm air.

Already the candleflies were glowing down in the dusky valley, and there were silvery tinkles from the tree-frogs.

'Won't it compensate?' Lucan had asked. 'The valley and the bay . . . for the giving of yourself?'

Kara could feel him on the horse at her side, breathing deeply and looking hard and male in his khaki knee-breeches and white shirt. She could no longer see his features, for the tropical twilight had fallen, but she could imagine the bold outline of his mouth.

A longing to be kissed by him shook her, to be held close and hard against him so there was nothing between them, no ghosts, no girl called Caprice.

Caprice . . . had he parted from her in Paris because his love for her was not to be borne in his brother's presence?

In the deep, enclosing tropical shadows they rode home. Lanterns were alight in the courtyard and there was a smell of hay from the stables that made the horses snuff the air. Lucan was out of the saddle before Kara. His hands found her and almost savagely he swung her down off the filly and close to him.

Wanting his touch, and yet afraid because

she feared he did not want her heart's love, she attempted to pull away from him. At once he caught her by the elbows and pulled her to him with impatience. The driving warmth of his mouth, the steam and smell of the horses, all combined to loosen the tension within her. Her hands clenched his shoulders, and then she let his wildness sweep her along with it.

When his lips released hers, she opened her eyes and saw his reckless look, his tousled hair, his nostrils flaring as he pulled air into his lungs. 'Well,' he said, and he laughed.

Kara drew back against a pillar that supported the stable beams, and her eyes were wide on his face. He had about him a look that reminded her of the night at Fort Fernand, when she had seen him returning from the card tables on the Scarlet Sloop.

'What am I to you, Lucan?' The words broke from her. 'A throw of the dice, a spin of the wheel of chance?'

'I suppose you could put it like that.' He struck a match and lit a cheroot, and his eyes through the smoke had a cynical glint. 'When a man takes a wife he stakes his liberty and he is unsure of the rewards. Yes, marriage is like a spin of the wheel of chance.'

Kara turned away from him and gave a

shiver as a breeze stirred through the stable-yard. From where she stood she could see the windows of a long room, and a gleam of ruby lamplight. A figure moved in the room, not upright like her husband but confined to a wheelchair. Her heart gave a curious jerk. Had Pryde seen Lucan kissing her from that window?

'I—I must go in and dress for dinner,' she said, and walked quickly away from Lucan.

*　　*　　*

Kara was dressing when there was a knock on her door. Her room had only one door, that which connected with Lucan's room, and she told herself she could not cope with him right now. She ignored the knock.

It was repeated. 'Oh—come in,' she said, and concentrated on attaching pearl bobs to her earlobes. The door opened to admit a houseman, clad in a jacket that was very white against his brown skin. He carried a silver tankard on a small round tray, and with a flash of his teeth he said that Massa Lucan wished her to have the toddy.

'Best rum toddy on the island,' called out Lucan without appearing. Jet came and stood in her doorway, massive and inquisitive.

'Thank you,' she took the toddy and because Samuel's eyes were steady on her face, awaiting her approval, she took a sip. It was delicious, she assured him, and he went happily away, leaving her door open.

'Estate rum,' Lucan informed her. 'With a finger of lime juice, a dash of passion-fruit, and a sprinkling of cinnamon. Do you like it?'

'Yes,' she said, and felt its warmth stealing to the edges of her heart, which quickened and questioned as he came and hauled Jet out of her doorway. 'I see you are not quite ready,' his eyes flicked her Greek-styled dress, which had a girdle not yet tied. 'Will you manage to find your way to the *salon*—the room with the double doors on the left of the hall?'

She nodded, and he closed the door between them and a moment later she heard Jet bark out on the gallery as he and his master made their way downstairs.

Kara finished her toddy and traced with her fingertips the dragon chased on the front of the tankard. The Savidge dragon was everywhere in this house . . . where the brides were so unloved that they either took a lover, or met sudden death on the Dragon's Stairway.

With fingers not quite steady she arranged

150

the folds of her dress. It was one she had bought in Athens while there with Domini for a few days of shopping. How carefree they had been! Domini looking lovelier with each passing day, made so by the deep love she and Paul had for each other. She and Kara had gone to a fashion show, where the dress had caught her eye. A soft, very feminine creation, unlike the casual clothes Kara usually wore.

White, embroidered silk and chiffon to the tips of her slippers. In it she was fragile, touching. She had meant to wear it when Nikos returned from America for the Christmas festivities. But he had not returned. He had written instead to say that he was married and would not be returning to Andelos just yet.

Kara stared at the delicate stranger in the mirror . . . now it was Maytime and she was married.

She turned from the mirror and gazed around her bedroom, dominated by the four-poster which Lucan had every right and every intention of sharing. The adjoining room into which she stepped was a dressing-room with a divan bed in it. Here his cheroot smoke lingered, and a tang of after-shave lotion. A handsome foulard robe hung behind the door, and dark silk pyjamas were laid out on the divan.

'The Wagnerian sword will not always share our bed,' he had warned her, and Kara took a deep steadying breath as she stepped out of the room on to the gallery and closed the door behind her.

The gallery was lit here and there by scrolled wall-lamps, and on her way down the staircase she paused to take a look at the golden lady in the window above the horse-shoe curve of the stairs. For a bewildering moment the golden figure seemed to have vanished, and then Kara realized that it was a trick of the shadows, they disturbed the pattern of colours that formed the figure and it was only in sunlight that she was clearly visible.

It was an illusion and no doubt gave rise to the superstition that the golden lady walked out of her frame and haunted the galleries of the house.

Kara gave a little shiver. This was a house that played on the imagination, with its history of drama and intrigue, its darkly panelled walls and alcoves. It needed livening up with music and laughter—a party, perhaps. She would suggest one to Lucan when she was more settled in and not such a stranger to everyone.

Absorbed in her thoughts, she didn't hear footsteps stealing up behind her. When warm hands suddenly masked her eyes, she cried out in alarm. 'Who is that?' She spoke in Greek, her natural language when frightened.

'Forgive me—' The hands released her and she swung round and found herself face to face with a fair-haired man who looked stunned. 'I took you for someone else— standing there you looked just like her—'

'Who?' Kara's heart was pounding.

'Now I see that you are not at all like her— it was an illusion of the shadows and the slenderness—'

'Who are you talking about?' Kara felt almost desperate to know.

'Why, Caprice.'

Caprice! Kara sagged back into the deep curve of the staircase. 'So you know Caprice,' she said. 'I have never met her, but I gather she is a close friend of my—husband's.'

He frowned, this thin but strong-looking man in the white dinner-jacket, whose fingers had felt so supple across her eyes. 'Now I understand. You are Lucan's wife,' he said.

'Yes, I am the surprise he brought home.' She strove to speak lightly. 'Pryde mistook me for Caprice, so he could never have met her?'

'She has never been to Dragon Bay.' He

had pale blue eyes and an accent that was almost unnoticeable. 'It was in Paris that I knew her, and where I met Clare Savidge. Clare was studying art. Caprice was working as a model, and I was trying to write the great Danish novel. I have still not written it.' His smile was self-derisive. 'Here at Dragon Bay I am tutor for Rue, and a masseur for the *seigneur*. He suffers the pain of cramp in the limbs he cannot use, and I was trained in Denmark as a masseur.'

'I see.' Kara smiled, and at once he responded, his features relaxing into a charm she was at once aware of.

'My name is Nils Ericsson,' he said, and he gave her a brisk continental bow. 'I am happy to know you, Mrs. Savidge.'

'Thank you—Nils. May I call you by your first name? I am such a stranger here, and it would be nice to have a friend.'

'I am good at being a—a friend.' Once again his smile was wry. 'Shall we go down? The *seigneur* likes us to be punctual for meals, and for everything else. He is like that, I think, because he has to regard his body as a machine which will run down if not attended to at regular intervals.'

'He strikes me as a man of great power despite his disability,' she said, as they walked

154

side by side down the stairs which had been carved out of the strong dark wood of a corsair galleon. 'He is stern and unconquered— Nils, how long have you been at the Great House?'

'About a year.' Nils gave her an encouraging smile. 'Does all its grandeur overwhelm you?'

She nodded. 'The Savidges themselves are overwhelming.'

'Even your husband?' he laughed, sweeping a side glance over her slight young figure in white silk-chiffon.

'I know it sounds naïve,' she met the fjord blue of Nils eyes, 'but Lucan is such a complex person. I feel that I know him less than I know you, Nils, and it is but ten minutes since we met.'

They reached the hall and turned towards the double door of the *salon*. Nils swept open the doors, and a log fire met Kara's gaze as she entered the room, warm and welcoming, evidently lit for Pryde because he would feel the cold more than other people. Its glow was reflected in the antique furniture and the glass fronts of the cabinets with gable tops.

'You are both a little late.' Pryde swept Kara with his grey eyes, taking in every detail of her dress.

'Time was made for slaves,' drawled the girl who sat with cool grace on the arm of a velvet sofa. She held a wine glass and was a slender, tawny-blonde with features so classical they made her look sculptured. Her mouth was lightly painted and scornful. She looked as though she had never had a warm emotion, and the blue dress she wore had the sheen of ice.

'Clare, meet Kara,' said Lucan, and he strolled to the sidetable where the decanters were clustered. 'Name your poison, Nils. My wife likes a small dry sherry.'

'A vodka and lime for me.' Nils put his hands in his pockets, and then withdrew them as though he were nervous of Pryde . . . or Clare.

Clare adjusted a pair of hornrimmed glasses and studied Kara. 'You are pagan Greek rather than classical,' she said, and her concise voice matched her looks. 'Your eyes are Byzantine. You must sit for me one day.'

'Don't be flattered,' laughed Lucan. 'Clare is of the modern school of sculpture and you will never recognize yourself.'

'Clare's work is recognized in Scandinavian countries.' Nils had that rigid look that concealed the charm of his smile.

'You Danes are a cold race.' Lucan handed

Nils his drink. 'I prefer something I can recognize as a human being, and a chunk of marble with a hole in its middle is not my idea of a woman.'

'You are old-fashioned—a throwback to the past,' said Clare, half indulgent. 'I wonder, Kara, that you did not run a thousand miles from this brother of mine. Savidge by name, savage by nature, that is what people say about him.'

'I am amazed at my own temerity.' Kara took a sip at her drink, and a glance at the man she had married. He had retreated beyond the ring of firelight and lamplight, as though his own strength was a burden in his brother's presence. But nothing, least of all shadows, could hide the casual grandeur of his body, the vitality of his hair and his gaze. As he caressed the great head of the dog at his side, Kara saw Pryde looking at him.

'That creature moped while you were away,' he said.

'He is just as fond of you, Pryde.' Lucan's hand withdrew from the animal's head.

'Nonsense. I can't provide him with exercise, and dogs, as well as women, like to chase at a man's heels.'

'There are exceptions, Pryde.' Clare's dress made a rustling sound as she leant forward to flick cigarette ash into the fire. 'I don't chase after men.'

'Clare would have us believe she is all art and no heart,' Lucan drawled. 'Those who work so intently have something to forget.'

Something . . . or someone, Kara thought, and she felt befriended by Nils on the arm of her chair.

'To men I am the marble and the stone I work in,' Clare rejoined. 'Could I be a slave, do I look a flower, am I made to be the muse of a man when I love the touch of cold stone?'

'You are a woman,' Lucan said wryly. 'Don't fight it, Clare.'

'Be a woman and enjoy "sorrow's sauce for every kiss?"' Clare gave a laugh in which ice seemed to tinkle. 'Happiness for me is involvement with my work, not with a man. Love? Love demands every fibre, every heartbeat, every nerve. I am sure Kara agrees. She is Greek, and they have always been a passionate people with a strain of sadness in them. Passion needs to be answered, and sadness to be assuaged.'

Kara was embarrassed, for everyone seemed to glance at her as though seeking the look of love in her eyes and on her lips. It was a relief when the clock chimed eight and the doors of an adjoining room were opened.

They went in to dinner, where at the head of the table a space was left for Pryde's wheelchair.

Soup was served from a sideboard supported upon a carved dragon, and the silver candelabra cast islands of flickering light between the diners.

'We must drink a toast to the bride and groom,' said Clare, and she held up her wine glass by its long hollow stem. 'I am going to quote Wilde because he was so deliciously wicked and wise—here's to "sweet things changed to bitterness, and bitter things that may be turned into joy."'

'One moment,' said Pryde, and he beckoned to Samuel and spoke to him in a low voice. There was silence at the table as Samuel went out of the room, and Kara caught Lucan's eyes upon her. Her heart beat fast, for what Clare had quoted was so full of meaning for both of them. Kara had known contentment, then disillusion—and now she faced a new, strange life that held undercurrents as deep and dangerous as those beyond the rocks of Dragon Bay.

Samuel reappeared and handed to Pryde the gold, dragon-crested cup of the Savidges. He half filled it with wine and handed the cup to Lucan, and he watched with piercing eyes as Lucan shared the wine with his bride.

'It's like a Greek drama,' Clare's laughter had a break in it. 'With all of us sitting at the family table, hiding behind our masks.'

'I am not one of the family,' Nils pointed out, and it seemed to Kara that he avoided looking at Clare.

'Well, you can console yourself with the thought that you are indispensable as a tutor—why, Rue would not tolerate any of those tame governesses that we hired.' Clare gave a laugh as she selected a beautifully browned cutlet from Samuel's serving-dish. 'That child has a Savidge temper.'

Kara took buttered vegetables from Samuel, and saw Clare glance significantly at Lucan.

The meal ended with mango in dry wine, and they rose to return to the *salon*. The double doors to the hall were open and a childish figure in a white nightdress stood in the opening. She was crying, the tears wet and forlorn on her cheeks.

'I—I heard her,' sobbed Rue. 'I heard the Golden Lady!'

CHAPTER SEVEN

It was Lucan who consoled the child with soothing words and hot chocolate beside the *salon* fire, and though she calmed down as she sipped her drink, her head resting against his shoulder, she still insisted that she had heard someone in a silk dress outside her room.

'It's all imagination,' Clare muttered as she lit a cigarette. 'She has more than her share of it.'

'All the same,' said Nils, 'it might reassure Rue if I took a look around upstairs. A bat might have flown in through a gallery window and the flutter of its wings would sound eerie.'

'I might as well come with you.' Clare followed Nils out of the room, a rather unsympathetic type of woman in Kara's estimation. One of those who could not see things with a child's eyes, or feel the insecurity of being a small person in a large, many-roomed house where the servants were superstitious. Kara herself had been affected by the tale of the Golden Lady, who was said to haunt this house in which she had been unhappy.

Rue, her small feet warming by the fire,

listened to Lucan's tale of an Irish princess. Gradually her green eyes grew drowsy and her head nestled sleepily against him, and as Kara sat looking at the two of them she was stabbed by a painful suspicion.

Rue's unknown mother had abandoned her as a baby to the care of the Savidges . . . and it could not be a coincidence that the child had eyes like Lucan and hair with a wild fire gleam . . . she even had his love.

Kara put a hand to her throat, to the pulse that beat wildly there. Pryde from his wheelchair—Pryde like a shadowed portrait against the velvet curtains—glanced at her, and surely there was a gleam of sympathy in his grey eyes.

'Are you finding us a rather overpowering family, Kara?' he asked. He dipped a spoon in the ice-water Samuel had brought him and let a drop of it sink the grounds of his Turkish coffee. His hands had a power and grace denied to his body; and his concise voice lacked the Irish lilt in her husband's. 'Will you join me, or do you prefer a milder coffee?'

'This is from the Blue Mountains of Jamaica, ma'am,' Samuel said, with his grave smile. She smiled back at him and he filled her little blue cup.

'I am afraid I have a hard palate to please,'

Pryde said drily. 'Lucan, as you see, has a boyish penchant for sweet things.'

Lucan quirked an eyebrow, for he was sharing Rue's mug of chocolate. 'And what happened, Yunk? Did the princess marry the warrior?' Rue nuzzled his shoulder and gave a sleepy yawn. 'Did they live happy ever after?'

'Yes, in their castle above an Irish glen, with the turf fires smoking into the cool evening air, and the princess making music at her harp.'

'What's a harp?'

'It's what angels play, my poppet.'

'And was the princess truly happy with her warrior?'

'Until they went beyond the sunset.' Lucan stood up, cradling the child against him. 'Come, little one, I'll take you up to bed—'

'No—' She began to struggle and the tears started to her eyes again. 'No, I don't want to be all on my own up there!'

Kara set aside her coffee cup and rose to her feet. 'I will stay with her until she sleeps.' She smiled at Rue. 'Would you like that?'

Rue nodded, and Kara was touched to her heart by that small, frightened face. She turned to Pryde to say goodnight, and he took her fine-boned hand into his and she felt the steel in his fingers, and gazed down at the face

163

that might have been that of Sebastian, the martyr of a thousand arrows.

'The young are imaginative and full of fancies,' he said. 'Don't allow yourself to give way to youthful fancies, Kara. This is a large house and it has seen a lot of history, but now we must all look forward to the future—to the brothers and sisters Rue will have in time.'

Kara pulled her hand quickly free of Pryde's. 'Goodnight, *seigneur*,' she said, and as she walked upstairs beside Lucan and the child she was sure that Pryde had not spoken figuratively. He had meant her to understand that if she had a child it would be the brother or sister of Rue.

Clare and Nils were talking on the first gallery. Clare swung round at the sound of footfalls, and there was a defensive glitter in her eyes. 'Oh, are you and Lucan off to bed?' she said to Kara.

'I am going to sit with Rue until she falls asleep.' Kara managed to smile at her sister-in-law, but at heart she was trembling, appalled by the thought of going to bed with Lucan, a man she did not know any more. A stranger to her, who had a beautiful girlfriend in Paris, and who might be the father of the child whom Pryde had adopted.

'Goodnight, pretty one.' Nils gave the child's soft hair a stroke. 'You are lucky to have such nice young aunt.'

'You are spoiled and indulged, Rue.' Clare's lips were drawn in tightly, and as she hurried downstairs her dress rustled around her like a coating of ice.

Nils' eyes held a wry expression as he gazed after her. 'There were no ghosts,' he said, but Kara shivered and felt the past all about in this house at Dragon Bay.

*   *   *

Lucan carried Rue into her bedroom, which was much too large and grand for a small child. Her night-lamp was still alight. Shaped like Aladdin's magic lamp it aureoled the big bed but left shadows lurking in corners and between the carved furniture. A child needed a room with light-coloured walls and rugs, Kara thought, and furniture of her own dimensions, brightly painted.

Lucan tucked the covers around Rue, who lay looking up at him, small and defenceless in the lamplight.

'Kara will sing you to sleep,' he said. 'She knows many old songs, but she is too shy to sing one for me.'

165

'But she is your wife,' giggled Rue, loving the attention she was receiving from him. She reached up and touched his cheek.

'Yes,' he cast a quizzical glance across the bed at Kara. 'And I am her husband.'

Kara, her nerves drawn as taut as a bowstring, watched the lamp glisten on the dark fire of his hair as he bent to give Rue a goodnight kiss. 'See you tomorrow, mischief.'

'See you tomorrow, darling Yunk.'

He strode to the door and from there he gazed back at Kara, tall and dominant, his eyes taking in her chiffon-clad figure. 'Just one song,' he said, and then abruptly he unbuttoned his dinner jacket, brought it to Kara and wrapped its warmth about her. 'The nights grow cold at Dragon Bay,' he added, and the next moment he was gone and the door was closing behind him.

Kara felt the warm weight of Lucan's jacket like an embrace. She wanted to throw it off, but Rue would have been bewildered, even hurt. 'Where are your toys, Rue?' she asked, for the room was so unchildlike, with not a doll or a paintbox in sight.

Rue pointed to a large corner cupboard, and Kara went and opened it. The deep shelves held a number of dolls and books and other toys, all tidily arranged. 'I'm not allowed to clutter,' said Rue. 'Da gets annoyed at untidiness.'

Da, who had been so annoyed with the boyish Lucan for being untidy. Kara took out a copy of *Les Fables de la Fontaine* and glanced through it. Suddenly her heart felt jarred, for inside on the flyleaf was written: '*Ma chère* Lucan, who has told me so many fairy tales.' The handwriting was feminine, the ink faded. The book was about eight or nine years old.

'Do you read these la Fontaine fables, Rue?' she asked, forcing herself to speak calmly, telling herself that before she had met Lucan she, too, had loved someone else.

Rue nodded. 'The book belongs to Uncle Lucan, but he lets me read it. I don't understand all the stories—would you read me one, Kara?'

'Not right now,' Kara replaced the book, and spun the sail of a painted windmill. She thought of the old, fire-blackened sugar mill and the shadow that had darkened its window as she and Lucan rode by. 'I have not yet met your Da,' she said. 'She sounds a martinet.'

'Da has a son she visits—she is treated almost like one of the family because she has been at the Great House for fifty years.' The awe with which Rue spoke was punctuated by a yawn, and as Kara came to the bedside she saw that the child was struggling not to fall asleep. She was afraid to be left alone.

Kara sat down on the bed and stroked a strand of russet hair out of the child's eyes— the green and drowsy eyes of a little curled-up cat, her lashes catching the lamplight and glinting with foxfire.

'What is a f-foundling?' Rue asked, and Kara felt a sudden painful urge to take the sleepy bundle into her arms.

'Who has called you that, poppet?' she asked quietly.

Rue bit her lip. 'Oh, I read it in a book. It was in *Daddy Long Legs*, I think. Does it mean my—my father didn't want me and gave me away?'

Kara noticed that the child did not say father and mother. It was her father who was important to her, and Kara wondered how much she had guessed or surmised from the conversation of the servants. Da for instance had been here for fifty years. She would know everything that went on at Dragon Bay.

'Sometimes,' Kara said gently, 'grown-up people do things they regret and some of them try to atone for any pain they have caused. As you grow into a big girl, Rue, you will under-stand better—' Kara stifled a sigh, for she didn't fully understand herself, or condone actions that caused heartache for other people. She was bewildered and hurt by the things she was learning about Lucan.

'Sing to me,' Rue coaxed. 'Uncle Lucan said you would.'

And softly, in the lamplight, Kara sang a Greek song of her own childhood to this lovely, imaginative child born out of a wild and fleeting love.

Rue stirred and lifted her drowsy eyelids as the song came to an end. 'Kara, don't leave me all alone,' she pleaded.

'Of course I won't.' Kara rose from the side of the bed and went and drew open the curtains at the big windows. The stars blinked in the sky like golden eyes as she turned out the Aladdin lamp and slipped out of her dress. She slipped into bed beside Rue and the child cuddled against her with a sigh of contentment. In a while she slept, but Kara lay wide-eyed in the starlit room.

She knew that if she had returned to her own bedroom she would have locked the door against Lucan. It was better that she stay here, where she had the excuse of being needed by Rue. She strove not to think about Lucan, but there was pain at her heart as Rue's silky hair brushed her cheek.

★　　★　　★

From that night onward a barrier arose between Kara and her husband which he made no immediate attempt to break down. He was away from the house for hours at a stretch, supervising the work down in the cocoa valley, and among the acres of banana trees. Green and tousled-looking trees, borne down by the great ripening hands of fruit.

Now and again Kara rode with him on his rounds, for there existed between them a kind of ice-hot truce; a game of make-believe they played in front of his brother and Clare: a charade that ended when they closed the door of their suite and shut between them the door of Kara's bedroom.

Kara never knew when Lucan's restraint would break, when the suave companion would turn upon her with demanding eyes, and so their rides together held a dangerous charm. Their beach picnics, often with Rue, held an underlying tension that tinged the hot days with a shadow of storm.

Kara and Rue fished with scoop-nets from the slippery rocks of Dragon Bay, and cooked their catch over a fire of sun-dried driftwood and seaweed. They sang as they toasted their

170

catch, a pair of sea-draggled urchins in shorts and sun-tops. Their driftwood fire smoked tangily and shot out flames as blue as the tropical sky.

The days were not unhappy. The sun felt good on Kara's skin as they clambered about among the rocks, avoiding the spiny sea-eggs and collecting clumps of rainbow coral and fan-bright shells. When Julius was about they clamoured for crisp, nutty coconut meat, and he went hand over hand up the incline of a coconut palm, his bare feet gripping its ridges, and lopped the nuts from among the leaves with his razor-sharp cutlass. The hairy brown nuts came thudding to the sun-white sand, and Rue said with bloodthirsty relish that they were like the heads of pirates hiding up the tree from fierce Julius.

Julius laughed richly, and Kara saw how he worshipped the child, and why. From their boyhood, Lucan had told her, Julius had been his own special Carib. There existed between them a bond that reminded Kara of that between her brother Paul and Yannis, the black-eyed Greek who had fought with him in the rebellion and who served him with such devotion.

Kara had written to Paul from Dragon Bay, and she awaited his reply to her letter

171

with trepidation. She had hoped that Paul or Domini would not read between the lines of a letter that was filled mainly with descriptions of the sugar-cane fields and the plantations.

'You catch a dusting I catch you, giving me that facety talk, man!' One of the cocoa workers went running by Kara, gay and brown and chased by a woman brandishing a twig broom. Kara laughed, for these people lived a rich life that had nothing to do with riches.

Each worker had his own house, with a plot for vegetables and a yard where pullets and piglets mingled with small children, who ran about in all their sun-dark nakedness. They were irresistible, with eyes like huge dark pansies, and Kara liked to sit on the veranda of the cocoa storehouse and be amused by the children.

Their mothers accepted Kara among them with a certain curiosity, but as the days went by they began to talk to her and to invite her into their colourful, food-spiced houses.

She was Massa Lucan's woman, and a dig in the ribs from a cigar-smoking crone was, she knew, the equivalent of a burning question. When could all the folks expect to see a boy-child at Dragon Bay? They knew, these earthy women, why a man like Lucan took a wife, and a certain wonderment shone in their eyes that their big fiery boss should marry a girl so slenderly boyish, with a face more elfin than pretty.

Spices sweetened the air; nutmeg and mace, and hundreds of bushy cocoa trees. The fruits of the sapodilla added a strawberry flavour, and there was a scent of grapefruit from the orchards of the Great House.

At night the songs of the workers echoed up the hillside, as they sat round the fires in the yards of their dwellings. Strange, primitive songs, and drums beating low like pulses, finding an echo in the heart of a slim Greek girl who was far from her homeland.

When Rue was at her lessons with Nils Ericsson, Kara took walks on her own. Today, feeling restless and a little homesick for Paul and his family, she wandered further than usual into the woods above the valley. Here grew the fairy bamboo which looked so pretty but was cruelly sharp and entangling, and here among the scarlet trees and the golden chain vines and parasol ferns ran the manacou, a swift little forest creature with the perky appearance of a squirrel. Kara knew there were snakes in the forest as well, that would lie as still as a branch and then strike out with the hiss of a lance.

With a wicker hat pushed to the back of her

head she wandered on, the bamboos striping her path, purple and white chalices brimming upon the vines with a wild, moist scent. She caught a glimpse of a green-bronze bird with a pendulum tail and heard his startled coo as she passed by. A king of the woods hidden among some trees dripping with scarlet tails.

The sun stripes grew wider and the trees less dense, and Kara guessed that she was coming out of the woods at some distance from the cocoa valley.

She paused on the path, feeling hot and pulling at the waist of her gingham dress. Nearby, at the base of a tree, she noticed a cluster of the flowers Lucan called touch-me-nots. She bent to touch one and watched fascinated as it closed its petals with a shrinking movement. It reminded her of the sardonic look Lucan had worn while showing her some of the flowers the other day. He had plucked a few and tucked them into the neck of her blouse, as if to remind her that he would not always tolerate a touch-me-not wife.

She hurried on out of the woods and saw that she was below the knoll on which stood the old sugar mill, empty and haunted, its bell still suspended in the arched opening of the turret.

The chirring of cicadas seemed loud in the

174

afternoon stillness, and Kara felt herself drawn towards the old mill as though by an invisible force. She climbed the knoll and smelled the rank grasses and old stone overgrown by moss. She pushed at the door and winced at the loud protesting groan of the single hinge on which it hung. The echoes were overloud in the dim ruin, cobwebs hung from the beams and patches of mildew stained the walls.

It was hard to believe that long ago flames had leapt under the abandoned sugar cauldrons, and a tumult of voices had added to the crackling of fire under the huge witch-pots in which the sugar boiled. An overturned sugar cauldron was said to have caused the fire in which Luella Savidge had perished, up there in the bell turret where she and her lover used to meet.

Kara walked slowly to the foot of the rickety iron stairs, winding upwards to a room haunted by an old, unhappy love. She was tempted to mount the stairs, up which flame had roared, belching a black smoke which had choked Luella to death. The young overseer had been out in the fields . . . he had galloped his horse furiously through the cane to the mill, and had tried to leap up the iron stairs to Luella. The sugar workers had restrained him. . . .

Kara pictured him with black smoke on his face, struggling to go to the girl he loved, listening as she tugged frantically at the bell-rope.

Suddenly the old bell moved again and the sound of it drifted down to Kara; a hollow little clang that made her go cold all over. She backed away from the stairs, her eyes fixed upon them until she reached the door. She pulled it open and ran down the knoll as if she had the devil at her heels.

She ran along a corridor through the cane, and her heart thumped as she heard behind her the thud of a horse's hooves—nearer all the time, real and menacing and not the hooves of a ghost horse. She turned to cry out to the rider to stop, and it was like a night-mare, for the big golden beast was riding her down, its great black mane hiding the rider's face as the horse reared up on its hind legs and brought its forelegs crashing down towards her.

She fell, pain shot through her shoulder and arm, and then the dust on the path filled her eyes and her brain and everything went dark.

*   *   *

She came to her senses in her bedroom at the Great House, and gazed up dazedly at the frilled canopy of her bed. She must have made a sound, for almost at once Clare was at the bedside and bending over her. 'Kara,' the other girl's face was strained, 'you gave us all a scare. How do you feel, my dear? Does your shoulder hurt very much?'

'My shoulder?' Kara was still dazed, and when she turned her head she saw that her left arm was out of the covers and resting on a pillow. It was also a queer saffron colour.

'You fell and badly bruised yourself.' Clare helped her to drink some cool lime juice. 'Lucan found you all crumpled up at the foot of the knoll on which the old sugar mill stands. He brought you home on horseback, and luckily old Doc Fabre was attending one of the workers and able to come in and pronounce you bruised but otherwise okay. You fainted, he thought, from a combination of shock and heat.'

'Someone chased me on a horse,' Kara said, with a shudder. 'A big golden horse with a black mane.'

Clare stared at her, as if the shock of her fall and the heat had affected Kara's brain.

'It's true.' Kara winced as she tried to sit

up. Clare helped her, banking the pillows behind her, her hands strangely cool against Kara's skin. Her clothes had been removed and she was in a sleeveless nightdress.

'I undressed you,' said Clare. 'The doctor wants you to stay in bed for a day or so. You suffered a nasty bruise, and your hat fell off and left you exposed to the sun—'

'I have not got brain fever,' Kara shrank from the odd expression in Clare's eyes. 'Don't you believe me about the horse?'

'There was once a black-maned palomino on the estate,' Clare admitted, 'but that was ages ago. He belonged to Pryde, and we got rid of him after my brother recovered from his accident but was confined to a wheelchair. We felt that Satan was too much of a reminder to Pryde of all the things he could not do any more.'

'Satan,' Kara whispered. 'He was golden with a fierce black mane?'

'Yes—' And then Clare turned to look at the door as it opened and Lucan came in. 'Lucan, come and comfort this funny little wife of yours. She insists that Satan reappeared this afternoon and rode her down.'

Clare gave a laugh, but Lucan was frowning. 'Will you leave us alone, Clare?'

he asked.

She nodded and left the suite. Lucan came to the side of Kara's bed and stood looking down at her, anger in his eyes instead of concern. 'You will not go near that place again,' he said. 'It's benighted and should be burned right down!'

'Someone chased me on horseback,' she drew back against her pillows, as far away as possible from his towering figure and his eyes that blazed like grey diamonds. 'I did not imagine it, Lucan. I was not sun-struck.'

'Did you go inside the mill?' he demanded.

She nodded. 'I—I was curious to see inside, and then the bell in the turret made a noise and I ran out—'

'And stumbled over a tussock of grass or a vine and fell down the knoll,' he said grimly. 'Kara, I begin to think that I did wrong to bring you to Dragon Bay—'

'Are you wishing that you had brought Caprice instead?' The words were out, the clamouring question was asked at last. 'You went to Paris to see her. You meant to ask her to be your wife.'

'Yes—I was going to ask Caprice to marry me,' he admitted.

Kara closed her eyes and wished that wing of blackness would sweep over her again, shutting out the pain, and the driving anger. 'Why did you leave her without asking?' Kara's great eyes were dark as shadows in her pointed face, her hair clustered in damp small curls at her temples and against her vulnerable neck. 'Could you not bear to ask her to take third place in your life?'

'Kara,' he moved as if to touch her, then thrust his hands into the pockets of his breeches. His shirt was open at his brown throat, and the look of him was a lance in Kara's heart. 'I thought I could ask Caprice to share my life at Dragon Bay, but when we met again in Paris I knew it was out of the question. I have known her for several years and she is vivacious, beautiful—but it was out of the question. Then—at Fort Fernand—I met you.'

'And it was easier, asking me to become a Savidge bride.' Kara spoke tiredly. 'I should like to go to sleep, Lucan. I am weary.' She closed her eyes, and a moment later heard him close the door. Even the fact that he had gone without further explanation was a source of pain to Kara. Her throat tightened and she felt utterly forlorn—and unwanted.

Tears started to her eyes—the easy tears of someone who ached all over—and she wished she had never run away from Andelos and the security of her brother's house. Here at Dragon Bay she was a stranger, bewildered and lonely. The one person who could have made her feel safe and secure had just admitted that she was not the wife he really wanted. She was second best, second choice.

Kara sought for her handkerchief beneath her pillow, and winced as the movement caused her shoulder to throb. Someone at Dragon Bay even actively hated her. A person and not a ghost had sat in the saddle of that golden horse with the satanic dark mane!

CHAPTER EIGHT

To her surprise Kara was inclined to welcome a day in bed. Rue came in early and perched herself on the foot of the fourposter, full of curiosity about the accident. 'I stumbled and fell.' Kara knew that this imaginative child must be told the lie that everyone else accepted as the truth. 'Silly of me. I am usually as sure-footed as a Greek goat.'

'It looks awfully painful,' Rue said sympathetically.

The bruise was like a rainbow this morning, spreading up Kara's forearm to the front of her shoulder. In throwing up her arm she had caught the blow that might have found her throat. A shudder ran through her. Someone was trying to frighten her away from Dragon Bay, but she must not think about that with the child in the room.

Instead she said brightly: 'I am going to ask permission of Pryde to paint the walls of your room a lighter colour. And we will change the curtains and put up something gay, and have a bright orange quilt made for your bed. Do you like orange?'

'Yes,' said Rue, looking eager and doubtful.

'And while we are at it, some of that big old furniture can be taken out. I am sure in a house this size there must be some smaller items of furniture.'

'I always think there is someone in the wardrobe—I hate that wardrobe, but Da says nothing must change at Dragon Bay. It's the tradition.'

'Things cannot help but change, Rue. The things that were appropriate fifty years ago are now heavy and old-fashioned.'

'You had best ask Da,' Rue said anxiously. 'Uncle Pryde leaves the running of the house to her, and she doesn't like things to be changed.'

'I should think your happiness comes before furniture,' Kara spoke with a touch of anger.

'It's different—if you are a real Savidge.' As Rue spoke she looked at Kara out of the corner of her green eyes. It was not her usual look of mischief, but one that held a secretive questioning. Kara bit her lip. She could not answer the child as she wished to be answered. She could not say, 'You are a Savidge; their blood is yours.'

'We have something in common, Rue,' she smiled. 'The Savidges *chose* to make us part of the family.'

'Are you glad?' asked Rue.

'Of course,' said Kara, and she and the child looked into each other's eyes and shared a secret. They both belonged to Lucan, but to neither of them would he ever really belong. They had to accept him as he was.

At that moment the door opened and Kara felt herself tensing . . . a tension that did not relax as Da entered the room carrying a tray.

'Ooh,' Rue knelt up on the bed, 'breakfast in bed! Can I have some?'

'Yes, poppet,' Kara was looking at Da, who always made her feel little older than Rue and about as responsible. The woman was still upright and commanding, despite her age. Her skin was dark, lined all over as ivory is when aged. Her eyes were quick and obsidian dark, set deep beneath her Creole turban with its devil-horns. The weaknesses of people were known to her and used by her. She had a power that made Kara think of *voodoo*.

'How is your arm this morning, ma'am?' she asked politely, settling the tray across Kara's lap and ordering Rue not to fidget.

'It aches, but I expect that will wear off. What a nice breakfast, Da.'

'Only one cup,' grumbled Rue.

'Hush, Miss Rue. You go and have yo' breakfast down-stairs like a good girl.'

'Let her stay,' Kara smiled up into the obsidian eyes that did not smile back. 'Perhaps Sam would be kind enough to bring up another cup? And look, I shall never eat all this by myself.'

There were *croissants* agleam with iced sugar, thick sliced ham, pineapple rings, toast, coffee, and fruit.

'You are the mistress here,' said Da, and she took a look at the chatelaine watch on the lapel of her long black silk dress. 'Massa Lucan tell me that Doctor Fabre call in aroun' ten this morning to see you, ma'am. When you had breakfast, I send up one of the girls to help you wash.'

'Thank you, Da. This arm is going to be a nuisance for a day or so.'

'It's all colours,' Rue had sugar all round her mouth from a *croissant*. 'I bet Yunk is mad enough to burn down that old mill— why, I bet the ghost pushed you over, Kara.'

Kara looked at Da, whose gaunt face was expressionless. 'You got too much imagination, Miss Rue. Folks all know that spirits can't push people over.'

No, thought Kara. Nor ride a person down on horseback.

Da went to each window and stroked back the curtains, and there was a look of fierce

185

pride in her eyes as she gazed round the room. 'This furniture was made at Dragon Bay a hundred years ago,' she said, 'and that marriage bed was built right here in this room.'

The marriage bed—how old-fashioned a term, how strong and abiding. Kara cut a piece of ham and carried it to her lips, and she saw Da looking her over in the big, carved bed with its frilled canopy and its big square pillows. Kara's heart shrank from the flicker of scorn in the obsidian eyes—for each morning the pillow beside her was as blank and smooth as snow, and bore no impression of Lucan's head.

'I will tell Samuel to bring another cup.' With a rustle of black silk Da left the room quietly closed the door behind her.

'She thinks she owns Dragon Bay,' said Rue, who was nibbling a pineapple ring on a slice of ham and toast. 'This is fun, Kara. I hope you stay in bed a whole week.'

'No fear—and, young lady, watch that juice. I don't want it all over my bedspread.'

'All over your marriage bed,' Rue giggled.

The entrance of Sam with another cup was a relief, and after he had gone, Kara said: 'Does Da's son work on the estate?'

Rue sipped her cup of coffee and milk and shook her head. 'He's a bit weird and lives all

186

by himself in a stilt house by the swamp. You haven't yet seen the swamp, but it's very mysterious. Sam says he's an *obeah* man—you know, someone who puts spells on people and makes love potions.'

'What nonsense,' Kara laughed, though she knew that a dark magic was still practised in these islands. Da herself had the look of a *voodoo* priestess.

When Rue had finished her breakfast, Kara told her to go and wash her face and agreed that she could come and eat lunch with her.

'You are a sport, Kara.' Rue gave her cheek a sticky kiss. 'Aunt Clare isn't like you. She is cold as a statue.'

'From whom did you hear that one?' Kara demanded.

'Oh, Nils said it to her once, when they were together in her studio. "You are cold as the statues you chisel out of stone," he said. Do you think Nils is in love with her?'

'You precocious child!' Kara had to laugh. 'Clare is very beautiful, but dedicated to her work as a sculptress.'

'I don't want to be dedicated,' said Rue solemnly. 'When I grow up I'm going to marry a man just like Yunk and I'm going to have ten children.'

187

'Only ten, my poppet?'

'You're laughing at me, but I don't care. I don't like playing all by myself, and I wish *you* would hurry up and have a baby.'

These words rang out as the door opened and Lucan came striding into the room. He paused, a bold eyebrow quirking above his green eyes.

'Yunk!' Rue scrambled off the bed and ran to him. He swept her up in his arms and studied her mischievous face before kissing her. 'Pineapple juice and toast crumbs,' he grimaced. 'Wash your face before you go up to the studio to say good morning to Clare.'

'Do I have to?' Rue took a strand of his hair and draped it in a comma above his left eyebrow. 'You are handsome, Yunk.'

'And you are a minx,' he said, his eyes narrowing. 'You will certainly go and wish your Aunt Clare good morning.'

'All right. Shall I give you an Eskimo kiss?' She rubbed her small nose against his hawkish one, and he chased her out of the suite and then returned and stood just inside the door of Kara's room. The lines of laughter etched deep the brown skin of his face. 'Minx,' he muttered.

Kara looked at him and wondered if he was thinking about the child's mother.

'Have you had breakfast?' she asked.

'A cup of coffee and some burnt toast at the overseer's.' His riding-boots creaked as he came across the room. 'Some rats have got into the cane fields and we'll have to see about getting rid of the pests. Can't have a good crop messed up. How's your arm—it looks as though Rue has been at it with her paintbox.'

'It aches.' Her throat had gone a little dry at his nearness. She wanted him to bend and kiss her, and yet she couldn't stop thinking about the things they had said to each other the day before. He had admitted that he wanted Caprice. How then could she, Kara, want his kiss? But she did, and her nostrils tensed as he sat down on her bed. The fresh air of the fields was on him, and the tangy smell of his horse. He took a sugar-apple off her tray, and his hair was wind tossed above his green eyes. Those strange eyes that changed with his moods—in coldness they were grey and he looked like Pryde.

He took a bite from the apple and then held it out with a quizzical smile and she took a smaller bite. 'It is usually Eve who does the tempting,' she murmured, a warmth in her cheeks.

'Are you prepared to be tempted?' His gaze was on her slim neck as he spoke, and his closeness was a subtle torment. She reminded herself wildly that he did not love her. He had married her and brought her here for one purpose only, and she saw a gleam of sardonic amusement come into his eyes at her movement of retreat.

'I—I am too bruised to want to be touched,' she said nervously.

'Sorry, my dear.' He tossed the core of the apple to the tray. 'I have made enquiries about the palomino you thought you saw, but Josh the overseer, and the other boys, say they have not seen one on the island since Satan was sent away. The golden palomino is a rare animal, and one with a black mane rarer still—'

'How would I know that Pryde's horse had a black mane?' she asked. 'That horse yesterday was golden as a new penny, with a fierce black mane that hid the rider's face.'

Lucan scanned her tense young face, and his nostrils flared and then drew in. 'I found you at the foot of the knoll, Kara. Your hat had fallen a yard away, and the sun was hot on you.'

'And it addled my brains and I imagined—this.' She gestured at her bruised arm. 'It's funny. Someone thinks you care about me—'

'*Kara. . .*'

'Someone wishes to hurt you through your beloved bride, Lucan.' She laughed on a broken note as he surged to his feet and stood looking down at her savagely.

'*Stop it!*' he ordered. He bent over her, one hand gripping the post beside her unbruised shoulder. His eyes blazed into hers, and then, as if to stifle her bitter laughter, he crushed his mouth against hers and held it there until she sank silent against the pillows.

She didn't open her eyes for several minutes. He was gone, the room was quiet and as drained of colour as she was. Her lips alone were achingly afire.

The doctor came, and later she had lunch with Rue, forcing herself to eat the crab salad, and the Angel's food—fresh sliced fruit with a garnish of grated coconut.

In the somnolent silence of the afternoon she lay listening to the whack of balls on the squash court. Clare and Nils, perhaps. Was Nils in love with that cool creature of marble? Attraction was a strange and subtle thing. A magnetic force that drew you to another person and held you there despite your misgivings. . . .

Suddenly she heard a distant cry and thought it came from the direction of the squash court. Later that day she learned from

191

Clare that a ball had hit Nils in the eye, and now he was wearing an eye-patch and looking like a Viking pirate.

'I don't know how it happened.' Clare paced restlessly about Kara's lamplit room, her cigarette spilling ash to the floor. 'First you have a bad fall, and now I give Nils a black eye—sometimes I believe those weird tales about Dragon Bay. Sometimes I almost feel a malevolent presence. Awful things do happen here. Look at Pryde!'

'Do you think Pryde blames Lucan for what happened?' Kara asked.

'My dear, they are twin brothers, made from the same block of marble. There might have been times when Pryde was—resentful, but he has too much pride to let himself be governed by an emotion that can't be controlled. Hate—like love—is such an emotion.

'Tell me,' Clare sat down and crossed her long legs, 'how did an innocent like you ever come to fall in love with Lucan?'

'It just happened.' Kara forced herself to smile. 'Did I come as a great surprise to all of you?'

'Yes,' Clare said frankly. 'He's a devil, Kara. There have been *affaires de coeur*.'

'And you don't think I am up to holding him, Clare?'

192

'I hope you are, my dear, because I find you sincere and kind-hearted—*Dieu*, that bold, bad brother of mine should have left you alone to play at sandcastles a while longer. You are a child! Little older than Rue.'

'I am twenty-one,' Kara laughed, 'and I am Greek. We grow up quickly in Greece, where it is recognized that a girl can best fulfil herself by loving a man—and bearing his children.'

'Love frightens me,' Clare rose in her restless way and went to toss the stub of her cigarette out of a window. She stood there, framed against the curtain in her dragon red shirt and tapering black slacks. 'A man's love is so primitive, somehow, and possessing. To think I am a Savidge—untouched by drama, a wild love, a destructive fury in my blood.'

She laughed as she spoke, but it seemed to Kara there was a false note in her laughter. She turned her gaze on every object in the room seekingly. 'This bedroom is large,' she said. 'I expect you would feel lost in it if you didn't share it with Lucan. And how plainly one can hear the sea from this wing.'

'Do you like the sea?' asked Kara.

'Not with passion.' Clare smiled, as though passion was something she kept at a distance from her life. 'The sea reminds me of love with its whispers, with its cruelty. I have my

193

work, and all else takes second place to it. With hard, clean marble I can fashion people as I wish them to be.'

. 'Cold,' said Kara, 'with no emotions to be wrung, no hearts to be gay or sad. You have your kind of people, Clare, I will have mine.'

'Yours will hurt you, little Greca.' Clare strolled to the door and opened it. 'Good night, sweet dreams—if such are possible in this house.'

Alone in her big lamplit bedroom Kara lay thinking of Clare and the things she had said. She denied the Savidge in her, but her roots were as interlocked as her brothers' in the history of this house; in the people who had lived here through the years of drama and feud; of love and hate. Their blood was Clare's. The impulses of her heart were surely as strong as Lucan's, or Pryde's.

It was, Kara thought, the elements of struggle in its occupants that haunted this house . . . and she tensed as she heard Lucan enter the adjoining room. She reached over quickly and put out the bedside lamp, and was pretending to be asleep when he opened the door of her room.

'Kara?' The light from his room plunged through her open door.

She lay still, and felt him with her every

nerve as he stood silent and tall in the doorway.

'Goodnight,' he said at last, and she knew as he left her in darkness that she had not fooled him. She buried a sigh in her pillow and wondered why she behaved in this way. Lucan was not a patient man, and in the end she would drive him right away from her . . . was that what she wanted?

All the miles between them that separated Dragon Bay from the Greek isle of Andelos?

* * *

Kara was too active a person to enjoy lying in bed and it felt good to be up and about again. Her arm was still an assortment of colours, but much less painful.

Lunch had been enjoyed on the veranda, and now the house was wrapped in its afternoon stillness. Nils and Clare had taken Rue for a drive. Lucan was out in the fields with Josh the overseer, and Kara knew as she wandered about the picture gallery that she shared the house with Pryde, who had wheeled his chair into his study after lunch.

She paused to gaze at the Irish brothers who had started the plantations and built the Great House. Conal looked a daredevil, but his brother had been rather dour. He was the

195

one who had not married, and something about his sombre gaze reminded Kara of Pryde. There was a similar look of autocracy, and a frown cleaving the straight line of the brows. The massive ring on Diarmuid's right hand was the one that Pryde now wore.

She wandered on, intrigued by the women whom the Savidge men had married. Some had been Creole beauties with high French noses and the look of queens. Others had been quite plain, girls married for their dowry, per- haps—or for the love that often flowers more warmly in the quiet heart.

Kara explored the long passages of the house, and mounted its sudden flights of stairs. She saw great chests in deep alcoves—looking like caskets—and as shadows began to creep along the galleries she came to the window of the Golden Lady.

As always, when the sun was not outlining the crinolined figure, the window looked vacant—as though Luella had glided out of it and rustled away in her golden silk to meet her young lover.

Kara shivered and found herself running swiftly down each curving flight of stairs, where at the foot of them she was brought up short by Pryde in the hall in his wheel- chair.

'You seem a trifle *distraite*,' he said in that attractively harsh voice of his. 'Has something frightened you?'

'The house is so big,' she said in confusion. 'Full of shadows and little creaks, especially when everyone is out and the servants take their siesta.'

'*L'heure bleue* is always a mysterious time. The blue hour, approach of dusk, when I enjoy a glass of wine in my den—the dragon's den, eh?'

She smiled slightly. 'I won't detain you, *seigneur*—'

'No, you will join me. A glass of wine will put the colour back in your cheeks.' He swung his wheelchair with expert ease and propelled it across the polished floor of the hall to the door of his den. The rubbered wheels pushed open the door and it swung back easily to allow him entrance.

Kara followed, feeling both nervous and pleased at being invited into Pryde's sanctum. It was a room of rich dark woods, glimmering crystal and flashes of ruby-red. Against the rosewood panelling were hung several of Utrillo's Montmartre scenes, soft coloured, softly shadowed. Kara knew at once that they were Utrillo's because she had once had a friend, an English painter, who had taught

197

how to distinguish the truly great artist from the facile craftsman.

Lovely paintings, Buhl cabinets inlaid with brass and tortoiseshell, and an ancient vase of Persian blue that made her want to hold it in her Greek hands that were so alive to beauty.

'Does my den please you?' Pryde murmured.

She nodded and sank down into the deep chair which he indicated with the lean, strong hand on which glinted the massive ring which each master of Dragon Bay wore in his turn.

He moved on silent wheels to a cabinet on which antique decanters shone lustrously. He poured an old amber wine into deep-bowled glasses, and placed a dish of sweet biscuits on the rosewood table between his chair and Kara's.

The brilliant melancholy of his gaze was upon Kara as she took a sip of the wine. The lamplight a little to his left was like a flame behind the ruby shade, and the tragic elements in his face stirred her, aroused a passionate pity, made her so aware of her own active limbs that she wanted to conceal them from this man who could not put his feet to the good earth and feel it.

'This wine is called *Flamme de Cœur*.' He caressed the crystal bowl with his long fingers. 'Do you find that it warms your heart?'

'It is like Greek honey with a pinch of spice,' she smiled.

'Do you miss your Greek isle?' he asked. 'Is Dragon Bay still strange to you?'

'Yes, but interesting. Your family history is such a colourful one, *seigneur*, and this afternoon I was up in the picture gallery admiring the portraits of your ancestors.'

'Each Savidge bride has her portrait painted. Your turn will come, Kara—a year from now, perhaps, when you have borne your first child. That is the tradition.'

Kara grew warm with confusion, and she glanced away from him and knew he was studying her averted cheek, her slim body, her shy-proud head with its flowing dark hair.

'Your portrait will be an intriguing one,' he said. 'You are a Boucher nymph in danger from a satyr. I see you are looking at that amber box—will you hand it to me and I will give you your wedding gift.'

'*Seigneur*, I don't expect a gift—'

'Of course you do, and I have been tardy in giving you one because I have not been sure of what you would like. Now I know that you like things of intrinsic beauty and not the show and glitter of the things that only impress other people. Please hand me the amber box.'

She did so and watched him turn the small key in the lock and open the carved box. He lifted a necklace out of one of the compartments inside. 'Very old amber,' he said. 'Tiny flowers of gold. Will you kneel beside me so that I can fasten them around your neck?'

Shyly she knelt on the carpet beside his wheelchair and felt the touch of his fingers against her nape as he fastened the clasp. She then sat back on her heels so that he might see how the necklace suited her. 'You have the skin for amber,' he nodded. 'It suits you very well.'

'It is a lovely gift, *seigneur*. I thank you.'

'I am glad it pleases you.' His hands clenched over the sides of his wheelchair. 'You must brave my den again and drink a glass of wine with me.'

'I want to be friends with you,' she said sincerely.

'Ah yes, friends.' A faint smile twisted one corner of his mouth, and she knew that he was thinking—what more could a stricken giant expect of any woman but her friendship?

She left him sitting alone among his rare possessions. The crest of lamplight illuminated his head and shoulders, the rest of him was in shadow. It would always be in shadow.

CHAPTER NINE

TODAY Kara had not found the courage to tap upon Pryde's door and invite herself into the dark grandeur of his study. Perhaps her reluctance had something to do with the way Lucan had looked at her at dinner last night—he had known the amber necklace was a gift from Pryde and he had not been pleased!

She paused on the Dragon's Stairway, and fingered the flower-shaped pieces of amber that hung warm against her neck. She still wore the necklace because she had been unable to unfasten it, and she had not dared to call Lucan into her room last night to unfasten it for her. His hands would have touched her . . . and shutting her mind to the rest she ran on down the giant steps towards the rippling water.

It had been a rather moody-tempered day and a sultriness hung in the air with the smell of seaweed. A lone bird swooped suddenly, cast a large shadow and was gone. She glanced at the sun, copper-tinged and awesome, and wondered if it was going to rain or storm.

She reached the sands and walked around the breakwater to the other cove, where a coral-stone beach house stood enclosed by a veranda. The long room inside was furnished with bamboo, and there was a cupboard of tinned provisions, a shelf of books, and oil for the stove and the lamps. Kara had brought cushions from the house to make the wicker divan more comfortable, for after her evening swim she liked to relax in the beach house for half an hour.

Eager for her swim, she stripped off her trews and her shirt and changed into her swimsuit. She revelled in the isolation of the cove as she ran down into the water. The shock of the waves was exhilarating, and she breasted them with easy strokes and loved the sting of the spray on her body.

As always in the water she felt free and unfettered, and took no heed of the stormy hue of the sun as it began to slide into the sea. It was like swimming in molten pewter, and the chains of coral that guarded the bay were alight along their tips. The raw smell of the coral was in her nostrils and the tang of the sea upon her lips.

The cawing of the seabirds grew louder as she neared the coral bastions—they were diving and feeding and as a greedy gull snatched a fish from the beak of another there was a wild flapping of wings and shrill cries that echoed across the water.

Kara turned at last to swim homeward, and saw a large, finned shape glide from an opening in the coral and show its long snarling snout above water. Kara's blood seemed to freeze for a moment. 'Don't ever panic if you see a barracuda,' Lucan had said. 'Swim swiftly for the shore, and don't try that silly trick of kicking about. It won't frighten the sea-tiger, and you will waste precious energy. Just swim, effortlessly and fast.'

Kara struck out for the shore, which was about half a mile away. A swift backward glance showed her the tailfin of the barracuda cutting through the water behind her. She was scared, for she knew that the beast attacked by tearing out a chunk of leg or thigh.

She knew also that she was not up to racing that monster with an arm that was still rather stiff, and she made hastily for a large rock that jutted out of the water and reached it just in time. With the energy of the desperate she hauled herself beyond the reach of the saw-edged teeth and huddled on the rock, watching with frightened eyes as the sea-tiger circled her small fort of refuge, showing its toothy snout and greedy eyes.

'Go away, you brute!' she said, and knew that it might be an hour or more before the killer-fish grew bored and swam off. She gazed towards the shore and wished Julius would appear. He would spot her with his keen eyes and come for her in his skiff.

'Julius!' she yelled. 'Julius!'

But only the seabirds answered, and the sea darkened and the presence of the circling barracuda grew even more fearsome. Kara shivered with nerves and increasing coldness, for every now and again a wave dashed halfway up the rock and drenched her with spray. The next wave came a little higher, and she saw the birds heading for the safety of the cliffs and realized that if a storm should start, she would be swept off her refuge into the jaws of the barracuda.

The wind quickened and the palm trees along the shore were bending lower. Vagrant spots of rain touched her cheeks, and a feeling of despair was creeping over her when she saw a movement on the shore and glimpsed the white shirt of a tall, dark figure.

'Julius!' She prayed wildly that he would hear her. 'Ahoy there! Ahoy—I'm stranded! *Julius!*'

The wind must have carried her cries across the water, and her waving arms might have been spotted in the sea light that still faintly lingered, for almost at once the man was running towards the skiff that was tied up by the jetty of the other cove. Kara thanked her stars as she saw the dark figure climb into the boat and begin to row out towards her.

Each wave now seemed to be trying to drag her from the rock to which she clung, and her hands and feet were growing numb with the cold. 'Hurry, Julius,' she pleaded through chattering teeth. 'P-please hurry.'

And then, as the skiff grew closer, a sudden flash of lightning lit the rower's face—strong, relentless, the face of Kara's husband!

More flickers of lightning revealed her slim, drenched, clinging figure to him, and then the skiff scraped in against the side of the rock and for a moment the savagery of Lucan's eyes were almost worse than the sea-tiger's.

'A—a barracuda was circling me,' she stuttered, chilled by the rain and by his anger.

'Into my arms—quickly!' She was caught and collected into his arms as if she were sea-drift. For taut seconds her wet, tousled head rested against his shoulder and she felt close to her the vigorous beat of his heart. Then he put her from him into the other seat and began to row through the rising fury of the waves towards the shore.

A dragon's tail seemed to lash at them, and Kara sat huddled on her seat, longing for some word of comfort from her grim-faced husband.

'You do the craziest things,' he said, the words lashing her above the rage of the wind. 'There was every indication that a storm was coming on, yet you swim out that far and risk attracting a barracuda.'

'I—I am so glad you spotted me.' She felt like weeping with distress and coldness. 'Julius is sometimes p-pottering about on the shore and I thought—'

'You thought it was he who was coming to pick you up.'

'You are n-not often home from work until l-later—' her teeth chattered so hard that she had to massage her jaws with her numbed hands.

'You little fool,' he muttered. 'You must have been out on that rock some time—good thing I felt like a stroll, or you would still be out there.'

'Don't!' she pleaded. The gathering roar of the stormy seas was all about them, the spray stung like needles, and through it all she was aware of the angry glint of his eyes. He never showed her any gentleness, she thought wearily. He never spoke a word that might betray worry or concern. He had decided to take a stroll, that was all, and she had spoiled it for him.

He had had to row out to bring her in, and now his shirt was plastered to his torso as the waves flung over the skiff and it took all his strength and skill to keep them from being overturned.

At last, after nightmare minutes of tumult and struggle, they were in against the jetty and he was leaping up and securing the bucking skiff to a bollard. Then he hoisted Kara out of the boat and began to plough through the wet sands, Kara in his arms. A tongue of wind and water lashed at them, and then he had made it to the other cove and Kara thought he would make for the lift in the tunnel. Instead he carried her towards the beach house, while lurid flashes of lightning lit the heaving seas.

'Lucan—the lift!' Kara yelled above the demoniac wind.

'No,' he shook his head, his hair in wet jags along his forehead. 'The electricity fails during a storm and we might get trapped halfway up.'

And as he mounted the steps of the beach

house and pushed open the door, Kara's heart beat with a new wildness. He dropped her to her feet, and the lightning flashes showed him the way to the table on which stood a lamp and a box of matches. Kara closed the beach house door and shut out some of the stormy din, and she blinked as the lamp bloomed, and shivered in her wet bathing suit.

'Get out of that wet thing while I light the stove and heat up some soup,' Lucan said briskly. He went to the cupboard of provisions and was examining the labels on the tins, his back to Kara as she cloaked herself in her towelling wrap and wriggled out of her wet-clinging swimsuit. It fell to the floor, and she stood hugging the wrap about her, unbearably conscious of her nudity as Lucan swung round holding a couple of tins.

'Tomato soup,' he said, 'and crab meat for a second course. There is also a tin of crackers and a jar of butter. Some coffee, too, but we haven't any water. We will have to make do with Rhum Clement—lord, you had better have half a cup of rum right now!'

He poured it and brought it to her, and she held her wrap together with one hand as she sipped at the potent rum.

'Don't leave a drop,' Lucan said sternly, and she forced herself to obey him as he set about lighting the small oil stove, and opening the tin of soup. There was a small saucepan in the cupboard and he tipped the soup into it and set it to heat on the stove. This done he turned to look at Kara, his eyes flicking her slim legs beneath the short wrap.

'Come over here,' he said. 'Where it's warm.'

She came and stood near the warmth of the stove, slightly dizzy from the rum, her heart in her throat as Lucan took hold of her, roughly, and began to rub her dry with the wrap.

'Don't wriggle,' his eyes glinted above hers, and she felt his hands on her body as he rubbed her down. Confusion and dizziness mingled, and she was glad when he decided she was dry and went over to the divan to get one of the rugs that was folded on the foot of it.

'It's a sensible idea to keep this beach house stocked with eatables and a few rugs. Here you are, wrap this around you—'

'I can put my trews and shirt on,' she said, with a dignity that was spoiled by a hiccup.

He grinned, and began to lay out biscuits, butter and pickles on a bamboo table. He opened the tin of crab meat, and the spicy aroma of the soup was filling the room as

Kara struggled into her clothes. She was zipping the waist of her trews as he came over to the stove to give the soup a stir.

'You still look as though I had caught you in a net,' he said.

She combed her fingers through her damp hair, and was smoothing her hair with her hands when she noticed Lucan's gaze upon her neck. There was an iciness to his gaze, a tautening of the brown skin over the bones of his face, and she only just stopped herself from hiding the amber necklace with her hand.

'The soup is about ready,' he said, and he whipped the saucepan off the stove, and Kara followed him to the table. Her face was nervously drawn, and she gave a jump as lightning knifed into the room and the jalousies shook in a peal of thunder.

'Close them,' Lucan said impatiently, and she did so, pulling over the jalousies the tropical birds and blooms worked in gay colours on the curtains. The room at once looked cosier, and she sat down facing Lucan at the circular bamboo table.

The soup was spicy and warming, and though his abrupt changes of mood were unnerving, she was glad to be in here out of the storm. Moths fluttered around the lamps

210

and beat their wings against the storm glass, and the smell of soup, rum and paraffin mingled to make a primitive scent.

'Do you think the family has guessed that we are safe in the beach house?' she asked, biting into a buttered biscuit piled with crab meat.

'I used to spend nights down here—in the old days. Care for another shot of buccaneer's cocktail?'

She shook her head and watched the rum glint in the lamplight as he poured a shot for himself. His eyes now were flashes of peridot, and his hair had dried into a sea-rough crest above his beaky features. He looked at home with a buccaneer's cocktail in his hand, his shirt open at the throat that was firm as teak.

Kara gave a jump as a tree crashed, only yards it sounded from the veranda of the beach house. The sea and the wind were howling together as if trying to outdo one another in fury. 'The poor old palm trees are taking a beating,' she said. 'Do these storms last long, or do they blow themselves out in an hour or so?'

He didn't answer directly, and she glanced up from her plate and caught the mockery in his gaze. 'It might be hours before this one blows itself out. It might last a night—who

211

knows?'

A night of storm. A night alone with Lucan. Her heart beat furiously, for here there was no door to close between them!

'Have some persimmons?'

He had opened a tin of the plum-like fruits, but her appetite was satisfied and she rose from the table and walked across to the book shelf. If they were going to be here for hours, a book might help to pass the time more easily. She studied the titles, then took one and sat down in a wicker chair. She opened it and tried to shut from her mind the fact that she and Lucan had not been alone like this since their wedding night in the forest.

'It is not the perfect, but the imperfect, who have need of love.'

She gazed blindly at the words as there drifted to her across the room the smoke of a cheroot. Lucan had stretched his long frame in a planter chair, and an hour ticked by as the storm raged on.

'You seem to have found an interesting book,' Lucan said lazily.

'A book of plays by Oscar Wilde,' she said without looking up.

'The wise and witty Irishman. The Irish, Kara, often mask their tragic souls with the blarney. Did you know that?'

'Are you trying to tell me that you have a tragic soul?' she asked.

He merely gave a soft and cynical laugh. 'I can ride a horse and row a boat, and go into the fields and cut cane with the men. I can walk the Dragon's Stairway, and hold a woman in my arms—but Pryde can do none of these things. He is the one with the tragic soul, eh?'

She thought of Pryde, surrounded by inanimate things of beauty, the lamplight on the ash-grey of his hair. She glanced across at Lucan and saw the foxfire in his hair.

'You do everything for Pryde,' she said. 'You give up things for your brother, but I sometimes think that you wish yourself a thousand miles from Dragon Bay, and that you only stay—'

'To salve my conscience?'

'Please don't make me answer that question, Lucan.'

'Why not? We are alone, surrounded by the elements. Never was there a moment more ripe for confession and the truth.' He swung his legs to the floor and leaned forward, the smoke from his cheroot narrowing his eyes. 'You regret our marriage, don't you? You find yourself tied to a man you can't love.'

'You talk to me of *love*!' She gave a scornful laugh. 'Must I love a man who loves another woman? I think not! I am a Greek and too proud for that.'

'*Pride!*' He surged to his feet and seemed to tower over Kara. 'I've had about all I can stand of pride. My mother had it—she was so certain that to be a Savidge was the next best thing to being a king that she let my brother and me behave like little tin gods. We rode wildly on half-broken horses; we played around with the heart of every girl that crossed our paths—Kara, do you think *I* was the only Savidge who ever did a wrong thing? Do you imagine that Pryde was always a martyred saint?'

Kara stared at her husband and saw a small raw flame flickering in the depths of his eyes. There was a look of barely controlled emotion about him, a leashed quality, and in the silence between them she heard the hiss of rain on the roof and the clamorous clash of the waves against the shore.

Was it the sound of the storm that drove her to her feet, or was it the raking look that Lucan gave her as she clutched the amber necklace Pryde had given her?

He walked to the door and for a wild moment she thought he was going out into the storm, then he turned and stood with his back to the door. 'That necklace belonged to Luella Savidge,' he said quietly. 'It was around her neck when they put out the fire at the old mill and found her smothered by smoke in the bell-turret. Did Pryde tell you?'

She shook her head, and suddenly she hated Lucan for telling her. She put up her hands and struggled with the clasp. 'Y-you hate him giving me anything,' she gasped. 'You are jealous of him—you always have been—'

There she broke off as Lucan moved. The room seemed darkly filled with him as with a terrifying violence he reached out and broke the necklace. The golden flowers scattered to the floor, and her nape was bruised by the broken clasp. She watched in horror as Lucan put his heel on the amber flowers and tried to crush them, and then like a wild thing she made for the door and wrenched it open. The wind and the rain blew in and she was about to escape when Lucan caught hold of her, and kicked the door shut again.

He spun her around like a doll, and never had she seen him look so devilish. A quiver shook her from her neckbone to her knees—she would have fallen but for the sudden grip of his arms. 'You are keen to please Pryde, eh?' he taunted. 'Very well, we will give him the one thing that he wants so badly—we will give him this.' The fire of Lucan's mouth was against her throat. 'And this.'

He lifted her and carried her across the room, and his eyes were purely sea-coloured and she was drowning in them as he put out the lamps.

★   ★   ★

The storm had spent itself in the night, and a deep stillness hung over the morning, not yet bird broken.

Kara stirred, and it was as though she had slept deeply in the hot sun and could not recall her name, or what bound her to the bed. Then she realized that it was a bare brown arm, and her fingers slipped free of the dark fire of Lucan's hair, as if burned. She gazed at his face as she lifted his arm from across her body. So still, so withdrawn, so that once again he was the stranger, the man unknown.

She slipped from his side and dressed in the dawn light—the curtains were open and blowing a little, and she remembered that when the thunder had died away Lucan had risen and opened the curtains and the jalousies. Then he had returned to her side and she had fallen asleep. . . .

She zipped her trews, and made her way out of the beach house, standing a moment on the steps to get a grip of herself. She swallowed the pain of the tears she ached to give way to, and walked away from the beach house, the heels of her sandals leaving a trail in the damp sand.

Moisture clung to the bushes of wild coconut, and over everything hung a veil of freshness after the downpour. The sea purred like a cat that had wrought mischief and was now lying still and innocent.

Becalmed, like Lucan, who had possessed her without mercy, without tenderness, as if anger drove him . . . anger that it was she and not Caprice in his arms. Remembering those hard, terrifying kisses, she hastened her progress up the Dragon's Stairway. The sudden flutter of a bird caused her pulses to race.

Lucan did not love her, and today she would pack her things and leave the Great House. A house divided because its loyalties conflicted; her slim body wanted only as a bridge across the chasm, to provide a son by Lucan, with hair like flame.

The sun began to rise and the sky flushed and burned like a bride's blush. She passed beneath the arching bough of the scarlet immortelle trees and there stood the house, gracious, wrapped in early morning stillness, the sun glinting on its many windows and mellowing its walls. A house built by love, and yet haunted by bitterness and pride.

She fingered her throat where Pryde's necklace had rested . . . where Lucan's lips had left a different touch. A scarlet petal dropped from her shoulder to the flagstones of the veranda, and she entered the spacious hall and looked about her with that sense of awe she had felt upon arriving here as a bride.

She ran her fingers over the smooth surfaces of antique mahogany, and as she walked towards the fireplace the great mastiff stirred and stood up. Usually he slept across the threshold of Lucan's room, but his master had been absent from the house last night.

'Hullo, Jet.' She stroked him and he nuzzled her with his great head, as alarming as a black lion to look at, but curiously docile towards those on whom he scented his master. He gave a slight growl, as if questioning her as to Lucan's whereabouts, and she patted him and smiled wryly.

'You ask no questions of him, do you, old boy?' she murmured. 'Your animal instincts tell you that you need never doubt his love, or fear it.'

She walked across the hall to the great staircase and Jet followed her, a big dark shadow behind her as she made her way to the Emerald Suite.

The rooms of the suite felt cold as she walked through them, and she glanced at the French clock on her mantelpiece and was glad to see that it would soon be time for one of the maids to bring her a cup of hot chocolate with cinnamon. She had caught the morning chocolate habit from Lucan. She liked to ride out in the mornings as he did, and she sighed as she threw open the doors of her wardrobe.

*   *   *

A suitcase was propped open on her bed and clothing was scattered about when she heard Lucan enter the adjoining room. Kara's heart skipped a beat, and Jet bounded into the other room.

'Hullo, old son,' she heard Lucan say. Then the door was pushed wide open and Lucan stood tall just inside the door. Kara felt him with her nerves, and knew his gaze was fixed on her suitcase and the clothing she was folding and packing.

'What is all this?' He came in a stride to the bedside.

219

'I am leaving you, Lucan.' She could not brave his eyes. 'Julius will take me in his boat to Fort Fernand—if you will allow him—and from there I can travel to Martinique and catch a plane for Europe.'

'Not Andelos?' he said harshly.

'Not right away.' She fought a trembling in her hands as she folded a dress into her suitcase. 'I wish to be alone for a while—'

'Do you really?' Hands gripped her shoulders, and she was swung round to Lucan. His expression was grim, his eyes cold and grey. 'Do you imagine I will let you walk out in this cool way—as though last night made us strangers instead of husband and wife?'

'We will always be strangers,' she threw at him. 'And if I have a child, Lucan, he will be a stranger to you. He will be brought up in a house of love—my brother's house—not here at Dragon Bay, where bitterness rules instead of love!'

There was a deathly silence, and Kara had no idea what would have happened if at that moment there had not been a sudden scream and a crash rising from the hall below.

Lucan stared down into Kara's wide, frightened eyes, and then he let go of her and hastened from the suite. She followed, nerve-torn, and when they reached the bend in the gallery they saw that a chandelier had fallen and broken into a thousand pieces on the floor of the hall.

Shards of crystal were scattered across the polished surface of the floor, and lumps of plaster mingled with shattered woodwork— then as the fog of dust gradually cleared they saw a small red-slippered foot and a small white-clad figure lying amidst the debris.

It was Rue. Elfin Rue in her Sunday dress, the sash torn from her waist and curling on the floor in the dust . . . scarlet as blood.

'*Rue!*' Kara's heart quickened with fear and her voice echoed it.

Lucan tore on down the stairs. Doors were opening, servants were running, and Kara saw Pryde sweep out of his study in his wheel-chair. His face was stern. Lucan's was anguished as he bent over that small, debris-smothered figure and began to tear away the lumps of plaster and daggers of glass.

'What has happened?' Clare appeared in her working smock, a smear of clay across her cheek.

'A chandelier has fallen,' Kara said in a voice that shook. 'Rue . . . the little one must have been almost underneath it . . .'

'Rue?' Clare whispered, and she swayed and went as white as her smock. The next moment she was running across the hall to her brother's side. He was lifting Rue, who lay very still in arms.

* * *

There was a hospital at Fort Fernand, but Dr. Fabre decided that it would not be wise to take a concussed child all that way. By road or river the journey was far from smooth.

As a plantation doctor he had a small X-ray unit which was often carried by van to the scene of an accident, and this was brought at once to the house and Rue underwent X-ray examination. There were external contusions, but, heaven be thanked, no sign of a skull fracture, and the doctor attended gently to the cuts and bruises the child had suffered.

'Let her be nursed in my room,' said Kara. 'I think she would like that.'

Kara knew as she spoke that Lucan would think she wished to put as much distance as possible between them. He didn't look at her when she added that she would use the child's room, and she hurried upstairs as the doctor attended to his small patient, and bundled into her suitcases the things she had been packing. Then she carried them past the window in which the Golden Lady hovered and into the panelled room which Rue disliked.

Kara unpacked her clothes and put them away in Rue's wardrobe. She couldn't leave at this critical time. She was good with sick people, having nursed her Aunt Sophula right up until the end, and Clare had said with a strained and helpless expression, 'I—I am hopeless with the sick and the hurt.'

Kara was sure that selfishness did not make her speak in that way. That small, bandaged, silent figure unnerved Clare, who was fonder of the child than she cared to admit.

On her way back to the Emerald Suite, Kara paused in the bend of the stairs and caught sight of Clare in the hall below, staring at the shattered chandelier, and then up at the ceiling where a great hole gaped, with torn wires curling out of it.

Workmen would be called in to repair the damage and to find out why the chandelier had torn away from the ceiling. Kara gave a cold shiver, for it seemed to her overwrought nerves that a sinister jester was at work at Dragon Bay.

She was about to continue along the gallery when she saw Nils join Clare and wrap an arm about her shoulders. Clare glanced up at him, and Kara saw from here that her face was strained and frightened. Nils bent his head and spoke to her, and as they made their way into the *salon*, a movement by the study door caught Kara's eye. A wheelchair glided out from the shadows. Pryde swung it around the pile of debris, and Kara wondered what his thoughts were as he sat looking at what had come terribly close to killing a member of his family.

Was he filled with despair because he could not climb the stairs to be at the child's side? Though lacking in Lucan's charm of manner with children, he seemed fond of Rue—so pretty, so much a Savidge with her alive eyes and vibrant hair.

As Kara entered the Emerald Suite she almost collided with Dr. Fabre. 'Ah, I wanted a few words with you, Mrs. Savidge. First let me take a look at your arm.' He did so, and pronounced it almost as good as new. Then he took a look at Kara's face, which was pale and anxious. 'The *pauvre petite* will need much attention in the next few days and I have the hope that you will be her nurse. I could send for one, but that will take time—ah, I thought I was not mistaken in you, *madame.*' He gave her a Gallic bow. 'You will take on the task?'

'It will not be a task, doctor,' she assured

him. 'Rue has come to mean a lot to me.'

Dr. Fabre nodded and fingered the stethoscope around his neck. 'I understand your feelings, *madame*. Rue is a delightful child, but then it is a strange fact of nature that such children are invariably above average in beauty and intelligence.'

Kara met the doctor's eyes, and she was wildly tempted to ask him if he had known Rue's mother. She fought the temptation, for instinct told her that the girl had been quite lovely, and so infatuated with the man in question that she had not counted the cost of loving him.

'Come,' said Dr. Fabre, and they entered the cool green room where Rue was tucked up beneath the covers of the fourposter. Lucan stood at the bedside, gazing down at the small face with its faraway look. Rue's hair was spread on the white pillow, and a bandage encircled her head.

'Will she be all right, Edmond?' Lucan glanced anxiously at the doctor. 'She looks so little and far away from us.

'She suffers from concussion and needs complete rest and quiet. I have asked your wife to be her nurse, Lucan. I hope you concur?'

Lucan glanced at Kara, but his eyes were

too brow-shadowed to be readable. 'Surely a professional nurse would be best,' he said.

'My dear fellow,' Dr. Fabre looked at him with shrewd eyes, 'you are concerned for the child and that is only natural, but I am sure your wife can do for her all that a proper nurse would do. I shall be calling in at regular intervals to examine the little one, who may remain unconscious for a day or more.'

Lucan gazed broodingly at his wife, then he turned away and walked into the solarium and Kara could see him looking down at the sea as she was given her instructions by the doctor.

Her answers to his questions were competent, and she told him about her aunt, who had been in her care for several weeks in the old Greek house above the harbour of Andelos. The house where Nikos had been born and where Kara had lived whenever her brother Paul was away on business.

Nikki had been deeply grateful to her for the care she had bestowed on his mother, and Kara had been too innocent at that time to realize that a man's love is not gentle or grateful or based on childhood memories. If she had known that she would have been prepared for Nikki's letter from America and she would not have run away . . . into the arms of yet another man who could not give her his heart's love.

*   *   *

The lamplight made shadows and the clock ticked softly. Kara sat in a deep chair at Rue's bedside, and the book on her lap lay open but unread. She was listening to the sea, which sounded strangely angry as it pounded the rocks of the bay. Rushing in, lashing at the lower terraces of the house as if seeking to take back what it had given long ago to the Savidges.

The clock chimed low and silvery, and Kara bent over Rue and laid the back of her hand across the child's forehead. Last night she had run a temperature, but tonight she was cool-skinned and seemed to stir slightly under Kara's touch. Kara sat with bated breath, hoping Rue would open her eyes and return to them from out of that world of her own.

Several minutes ticked by, but her lashes did not lift. Such long lashes, their tips curling upwards with a glint of bronze to them— the very same glint that Lucan's had when he slept.

She was filled with the memory of Lucan at

the beach house, the rage of the storm, the flash of the lightning, getting into his eyes and into his kisses until she had not known what she said to him, or felt for him. He was like a demon lover from whom there was no escape. She had thought to escape, but here she sat beside the child he loved so much, and when they met or talked there was between them a state of truce. He knew she would go when Rue recovered. She knew he would try to stop her—not out of love but because she might have his child, and that child might be a boy.

She forced her thoughts away from him and glanced around the green room, which she had transformed with the toys she brought from Rue's cupboard that afternoon.

Da had sat with Rue while Kara took a nap on the bed in Rue's room. After a shower and change of dress she had ransacked the toy cupboard and brought an armful to the Emerald Suite. Da had looked at her with sharp eyes embedded in wrinkles and high cheekbones.

'This a sickroom, Miz Kara,' she had said. 'You cain't put all them toys around.'

'Rue will see them when she comes to herself and they will help her to forget the terrible thing that happened to her.' And ignoring Da and her pursed lips, Kara had

228

proceeded to arrange the dolls and soft toys so they were holding out their arms to Rue.

'You like a child yo'self,' Da had muttered, and as she went out of the room the points of her Creole turban had seemed like the devil's horns.

Kara fingered the cherry-coloured ribbons of her quilted robe, and then noticed that one of the dolls had fallen on its face. She went over to straiten it, a favourite of Rue's with its stuffed body and limbs, painted face and impossibly red plaits. Ginger, she called the doll. Yunk had given it to her a long time ago and she often took it to bed with her.

Kara took hold of the doll to prop it against the dressing table mirror, and she gave a sudden gasp of pain as something pierced her hand. After sucking the pinprick, she examined the doll with caution and found the pin sticking through its head. She withdrew it and found that it was a sharp-pointed bodkin, which could have been used for sewing the doll and might have got lost inside it when it was stuffed.

A bare bodkin, impaling the head of a doll Rue loved. Rue, who lay so still and hurt, her bright head bandaged.

The clock ticked, the sea churned and lashed at the rocks of Dragon Bay, and Kara wanted to snatch up Rue and run with her from this house of menace.

With hands that shook she bundled the doll and the bodkin into the back of a drawer and slammed it shut. Then she hurried back to Rue and stood over her in a protective attitude. Long ago witches had stuck pins in dolls, and an element of superstition still held sway over the people of this island. What if someone in this house wished harm on those close to Lucan? Someone who hated him and blamed him for Pryde's accident. Someone who had frightened Rue at night, ridden Kara down in the cane, and caused the chandelier to fall.

Kara suddenly wanted Lucan. She wanted him in this room, his strength a barrier against that stalking someone who might at this moment be out on the gallery.

She straightened and listened, and her heart jumped into her throat as she heard the approach of footsteps. They paused, the room next door was entered. . . .

'Lucan?' His name broke from her.

The communicating door opened and he strode in, tall, a dark green sweater to his chin, carrying a pair of steaming tankards. His eyes as he looked at her seemed to collect the lamplight into them and become lambent.

'I thought you might like a hot rum punch.' He handed her one of the tankards, and then stood looking down at Rue. 'Still no change?'

'A little while ago she seemed to stir when I touched her.' Kara cradled the tankard in her hands and took a grateful sip of the spicy punch. The shadows of a moment ago were not to be feared when Lucan stood by to guard that small figure. 'Stroke her hair, Lucan. I am sure she knows when you are here.'

His large hand was curiously gentle on the wings of bright hair. The child's lips seemed to move, as if to murmur his name, and Kara knew beyond any doubt that the affinity between these two was of the blood, the senses, the very fibres of the heart. Why then had he let Pryde adopt what was his? Was it written in stone, or in Lucan's heart blood that he must give everything to Pryde? Was that why he had made such angry love to her, breaking the amber beads as if he longed to break free of his brother's house?

He stood by the night-lamp drinking his punch and there was something remote and melancholy about his profile. Kara was moved to touch him, to speak, but what after all could she say? She, who had sworn that if she had a child she would rear it as a stranger to him.

He kept her company through this second night and towards dawn, as she nodded in her chair, he made her go and take a rest on the divin in his room. Some time later he came to her, his hands warm on her shoulders 'Wake up, Kara!' There was a note of urgency in his voice. 'Rue's eyes are open, but she doesn't seem to know where she is.'

He half lifted Kara off the divin and almost before her feet were in her slippers he was hustling her into the adjoining room. Yes, the child's eyes were open, green and hazy as moss with the dawn dew on it. Eyes that gazed without recognition at Kara, dwelt thoughtfully on Lucan, then took in slowly the green-canopied bed, the wide windows filled with sea-light, and the dolls and lop-eared soft toys on the dressing table and other articles of furniture.

'Ginger,' she murmured.

No, Kara wanted to cry out. No, my dear, not that doll! Then Lucan shot a look at her, as if feeling her tension, and with clumsy hands she opened the drawer in which she had bundled the doll and took it out. She saw Lucan frown, and her hands were feeling all over the doll, desperately, as she walked to the bed with it.

'Ginger!' Rue reached for it with a smile of delight, and Kara had to give it to her and watch the child clasp it to her.

'She remembers the doll,' Lucan said, still frowning and puzzled.

'It is probably a temporary amnesia,' Kara reassured him.

Dr. Fabre was in complete agreement with Kara when he called in later that morning. The shock, he said. The blows caused by the falling plaster. It was little short of a miracle, *hein*, that the little one had not caught the full impact of the chandelier?

That russet-haired child, playing so innocently with her doll, would have been killed. The unspoken words hung in the air, and Kara saw Lucan glance about him with a trapped, leashed expression. He sensed like a wild, proud animal the danger in the air, and as yet he could not tell from what direction it came.

'Kara,' he said, after the doctor had gone, 'come in here a moment.' He drew her into the solarium, and the scent of the sea and the plants was a trifle dizzying. She sank down in one of the wicker chairs and was unaware of how small she looked, how large her eyes, how fragile and at the same time how indomitable she was. Kara Stephanos, in whom ran the

233

blood of Greeks who had fought tooth and nail for what they loved.

A fine mist drifted over the sea below the solarium—on a morning such as this her brother had almost died, and she had sat with Domini through the waiting hours.

She glanced up at Lucan, this tall, bold-featured man who was her husband, and saw her tiny image reflected in his eyes as he bent down to her and rubbed some warmth into her cold hands. 'I want to thank you for the way you care for Rue,' he said, and his words were almost an echo of those used by Nikos a year ago. Words that sent a warning to heart; words that armoured her against this man who looked so troubled, so uncertain, so like a lost boy whose tousled hair needed stroking back from green eyes guarded by lashes with bronze tips to them.

'Will you stay with her as much as possible?' he asked, and she felt him fingering the gold band on her left hand. 'My sister will sit with her while you rest—Clare owes me that,' he added in a lower tone.

'Now Rue is so much better, Clare will not be so—so unnerved by her. Clare is an artist and imaginative, and such people are never very good in sickrooms.' Kara looked at him and felt her heart beat fast. Dare she confide in him about the doll she had found with a bodkin impaled in it? Or would he think that she was being overimaginative? After all, it was bizarre to suggest that someone in the house was playing such tricks . . . using black magic.

Then the moment for telling had passed as there arose from the courtyard the impatient nicker of his stallion, saddled and ready for him to ride to the mill, where some new machinery was due in. The ring of hooves on the cobbles, the deep bark of the hound who always rode with him, drew Lucan's attention to the time.

'I must be off,' he said, and he drew Kara to her feet and held her by the elbows as if to pull her into his embrace. But all he did was to brush an impersonal kiss across her cheekbone. Then he strode into the bedroom to Rue.

'I will see you later, *petite amie*,' Kara heard him say.

She touched her cheek where the passing warmth of his lips still lingered. Little sweetheart! Her eyes filled with tears. Little Rue. I must not mind that he loves you, and does not love me, she told herself with firmness.

During the next few days Rue grew much stronger. Her partial loss of memory was due, said the doctor, to her subconscious wish to blot out the moment when the chandelier had come crashing down towards her. Her mind needed a cushion to rest against and so it chose to make blank the things she could not yet face.

She told Kara that she had dreamed of falling off her swing. 'Is that how I got hurt?' she asked.

Kara thought it expedient to say yes. 'Come, eat your breakfast,' she coaxed. 'If you eat every bit, then Dr. Fabre will let you get up for a few hours.'

The child's appetite was jaded and Kara tempted her patiently with chocolate in a cup painted with birds, and scrambled egg with curls of pink ham. 'Come on, cuckoo, open your mouth and let me pop in another titbit.'

The game proceeded until most of the plate was cleared, and then Kara set about straightening the room while Rue put on her heart-shaped wristwatch and the necklet of vari-coloured shells which Julius had made for her.

'I am an Irish princess and now I am ready

236

to receive homage from all my subjects. Bow to me instantly, you peasants.' She flattened her knees and her row of dolls fell on their faces and she laughed with delight, her green eyes brighter than they had been for several days.

When Kara glanced over and smiled at her, she said:

'Do you think I am like my father to look at?'

Kara's heart skipped a beat, for since her accident the child called Lucan her father. At first she had not known who Kara was, and upon being told that Kara was Lucan's wife she had said: 'Did my own mother die a long time ago, and was my father sad for a long, long time before he married you, Kara?'

'Well, darling, that is a question I don't like to ask him,' Kara had replied.

'I suppose you keep wondering if he loved her better than he loves you.' The childish candour had hurt without meaning to. 'You are very good and kind, Kara. I expect my father married you for that reason.'

'I expect he did,' Kara said drily, and suggested that they do a jigsaw puzzle.

Whenever the child broached the subject of her parents, Kara found a way to divert her. This morning she suggested that Rue try her legs out of bed and if she felt strong enough they would go downstairs and sit in the Folly.

The Folly was attached to the veranda, and it would do Rue good to sit in the sunshine for a couple of hours.

'I feel a bit wobbly,' she admitted.

'Sam can carry you downstairs.' Kara helped her to dress, and was glad that the debris from the broken chandelier had been carted away and the ceiling replastered. The workmen had found a crack in the ceiling, and because of the closeness of the house to the sea Lucan had suggested to Pryde that an expert on land erosion be called in to examine the cliffs on which the house was built.

'Those cliffs hold firm as iron in the seabed,' Pryde had scoffed. 'This house will stand another hundred years or more.'

'How can you be so certain of that?' Lucan had demanded with impatience. 'We all know that the sea is closing in, and the foundations of this house must receive a hammering each time the seas are high. I am darned certain that storm the other night had something to do with that chandelier breaking loose.'

'Old houses will creak and crack.' Pryde had eyed his pacing brother with sardonic eyes. 'Very well, call in an expert if it will put your mind at rest.'

238

Lucan was very restless these days—turning up at odd hours, looking in on Rue, then riding off again with Jet bounding beside him and baying down the cocoa valley.

The atmosphere was tense as if a storm brewed, and it was as much of a relief to Kara to get out of the house as it was a change for Rue. Walking behind Sam and the child, her arms laden with books, puzzles, and the red-plaited doll, Kara watched anxiously to see if Rue glanced up at the ceiling where the chandelier had hung. But no, she went on chatting to Sam and seemed quite unaware that here in the hall, ten days ago, she had been knocked out by flying plaster and had lain still and bleeding in Lucan's arms.

There was a smouldering murmur of bees as they entered the Folly, whose outside walls were a mass of clambering coral flowers. Inside it was cool and there were chairs set round the small fountain, a figure of Pan blowing water through the pipes he held.

Kara felt a lifting of her spirits and knew that something in the house had been weighing them down.

'Catch!' Rue tossed her ball to Kara, and then ran to the edge of the fountain as a dragonfly flew in and settled on the figure of Pan.

'Her wings are like green tissue and she quivers all over,' the child whispered. 'Kara, isn't the world full of lovely things?'

'Yes,' Kara said softly, and watched the sun slant in on the child's russet hair and stroke her young cheek.

'Kara,' Rue swung round from the fountain rim and her eyes were green as the wings of the dragonfly, 'don't you think that the Great House is like a palace? An enchanted palace, with a dragon and a prince and all of us under a spell.'

'What sort of a spell?' Kara asked indulgently.

'I am not sure,' Rue said thoughtfully. 'Do you know the story of the princess and the frog? He was a nobleman who had been enchanted and he knew that if the princess fell in love with him, he would change and be handsome again.'

'And did the princess fall in love with him?' Kara asked.

'I s'pose so.' Rue bent and tickled a darting fish. 'Fairy tales always end happily, but I bet it's different in real life. I mean, can you imagine a girl falling in love with a dragon?'

'A frog,' Kara corrected.

'Well, a frog is a little dragon,' Rue pointed out. 'Didn't you know that?'

'I do now.' Kara smiled and lay back in her lounger and hummed a few bars of a Greek song she was fond of.

'I like that,' Rue said eagerly.

'If I had a guitar I could play it to you.'

'Sing it, Kara.'

'Oh, I have not sung a Greek song in such a long time—'

'Please!' Rue ran to her and knelt on the foot of the lounger. She caught at Kara's left hand and swung it so the pearl of Lucan's ring gleamed with a myriad colours. 'Sing me the song, Kara. After all, I have been sick and you have to pamper me.'

'The Irish,' Kara murmured, 'have the charm of angels and devils—very well, you will have to clap, like this, because it is a song that echoes the rhythm of the olives as they drop into the big baskets of the olive pickers.'

They were lost in the fun of their concert when a shadow fell suddenly across the doorway of the Folly. It lingered for several minutes, while the young voices floated out into the sunlight, then the shadow withdrew and there was no sound of footsteps as it moved silently away.

'Kara, you must teach me to speak Greek,' Rue said excitedly.

'That would take a long time, poppet.'

Kara kissed the small hand she held and touched her forehead to it. 'That is the Greek way of saying "bless you".'

'Kara,' Rue gazed at her with eyes that were suddenly alarmed, 'you will be here a long time—won't you?'

'Of course.' Kara could not bear that look in the child's eyes. 'Look, when Sam brings our ice cream we will have some fun with him and you will thank him in Greek. This is how you say it—'

She held the slight figure in the circle of her arm, bird-boned and warm as a kitten, and tried to recapture her mood of gaiety. But it was as though a shadow had passed over the sun, and she heard a wind whisper through the fields of cane, and the chain of bells and coral hanging in the doorway of the Folly gave a tinkle as though something passed by.

She glanced up and watched the bells tinkling and swaying.

When Sam arrived, carrying goblets of avocado ice cream on a tray, Kara asked him if the seas were high.

'Them waves got a wind on their backs a-driving them, ma'am,' he said. 'That ole dragon is growling—'

There he broke off and watched with a grin

242

as Rue tucked into her ice cream. He ambled away, but his words stayed with Kara.

That old dragon is growling.

CHAPTER TEN

A FEW nights later Kara awoke suddenly and heard the neighing of a horse quite close to the house. Its hooves clattered on the cobbles below, and she sat up, listening. She knew that Lucan sometimes went out moon riding, but this was the middle of the night.

She slipped out of bed and the moonlight framed her as she stood at the window trying to catch a glimpse of the horse and rider. But from the window of Lucan's dressing room, which she was now using while he slept elsewhere, it was difficult to see anyone down in the courtyard. She hesitated, then slipped into her robe and slippers and made her way out to the gallery, where the moonlight streamed through the windows at either end.

Silently as a ghost, she hurried to the window that overlooked the courtyard. She heard again the rattle of harness and the stamp of hooves, and then her breath caught in her throat as she saw the big horse standing riderless, tossing its black mane and glistening in the moonlight as though painted with gold.

A beautiful, satanic-looking beast, glancing wickedly sideways as a figure clambered into the saddle and urged him through the gateway on to the road.

Kara's heart was pounding, for the rider was big, broad-shouldered, and tilted well down over his face was a field hat with a wide brim—a hat such as the one Lucan often wore!

The sound of the galloping hooves died away into the night, and Kara stood shivering on the gallery. Had she just seen Lucan on a golden horse with a black mane, or was she walking in her sleep and having a nightmare?

If she had seen Lucan, then it was he who had ridden her down in the cane—he who played some terrible underhand game at Dragon Bay. Lucan, her husband, who ten years ago had been alone with Pryde when he had fallen from the cliffside and broken his back.

She wanted to hasten to the room where Lucan had been sleeping for the past week, and yet she hesitated. What if she opened the door and came face to face with its emptiness? Could she bear knowing that he had been her mysterious assailant? Could she stay, even for Rue's sake, knowing that Lucan plotted to harm her because he found her a tiresome

245

mistake?

She stood forlorn and ghostly on the moon-lit gallery, then she fled back to her room and closed the door hurriedly behind her. She crept into bed and lay cold and trembling. She closed her eyes and wanted to fall into the abyss of sleep, but there in her mind's eye she saw again that tall figure on horseback. There was little doubt in her mind that she had seen Lucan!

Kara wondered in the next few days if he guessed that she was avoiding being alone with him. When he came in from the fields he always managed to be downstairs with Rue. He would go up for a shower and when he came down again, it would be time for Kara to take Rue upstairs to bed. She would hang out the time until dinner, reading to Rue from the book of la Fontaine fables; the book with another woman's handwriting in it.

Ma chère Lucan.

At dinner she would feel fairly secure with Pryde at the head of the table, and Clare and Nils facing her. Tonight Clare looked thin and striking in a black velvet dress with a silver-webbed topaz on the left shoulder. She talked brilliantly about art, travel, and her favourite cities. Nils, Kara noticed, was very quiet. There was a withdrawn air about him, as though he had received a recent blow that was hurting him.

Was it a blow caused by Clare? Nils was in love with her, but for Clare love was too possessive, too demanding. She wanted to be free. Nils was a man who cared for children and he would not want a wife who preferred images to warm, laughing, mischievous realities.

Poor Nils! Kara smiled across at him to let him see that she understood and in a way was in the same unhappy boat.

The Savidges were not easy to understand or love—strong and wilful people were never as easy to love as the gentle and placable.

'I like your beads, Kara.' Clare was leaning forward to look at them in the light of the dining candles. Several loops of silver beads with a Greek letter stamped on each bead. Worry beads that spelled a prayer.

'They were given to me by my aunt, a fierce little Greek lady,' Kara smiled.

'They're worry beads,' Clare said quietly. 'Are you wearing them as an adornment or to help soothe away a worry of some sort?'

'Oh, to be adorned.' Kara felt Lucan looking at her and she strove to speak lightly. 'Your brooch fascinates me, Clare. Is it a spider in a web?'

'Wickedly cute, isn't it?' Clare laughed.

247

'Some people would say symbolic.' Lucan was looking across at his sister as he carried his wine glass to his lips.

'Am I the only one caught in a web?' she asked. 'Aren't we all?'

'All of us at Dragon Bay?' He quirked the eyebrow that made him look devilish.

'Yes, that was what I meant.' She glanced at Pryde, who was cracking nuts with deliberate movements of his strong and beautiful hands. Hands, Kara noticed, that were more powerful than one would expect an invalid's to be.

'Pryde,' there was a sudden note of torment in Clare's voice, 'don't you ever rebel at the web which fate has spun for you?'

'Fate, my dear,' he lifted his gaze from the nutcrackers and the candlelight reflected like points of flame in the full, black pupils of his eyes, 'does not weave the traps into which we fall. I think we weave them for ourselves by putting too much trust in the affection we feel for others.'

Kara felt as though a draught passed across the nape of her neck, stirring the small hairs. Pryde and his twin had been like one person, until Lucan had realized that Dragon Bay and all it stood for were Pryde's to inherit, his to merely serve. A challenge had been made, and Pryde had taken a fall from which he would never rise to walk again.

She gazed at Pryde, whose breadth of shoulder was heavier than Lucan's, without the lean, athletic slope to the hips. Had that slight heaviness, that squareness to the waist always been present? If so, then Lucan would always have been the fleetest of the two; the more adept at swimming, riding—and climbing.

Later in the *salon* Lucan asked her to play for them. She went to the piano without looking at him and raised the lid. 'What would you like me to play, Pryde?' She turned on the stool and smiled across at her brother-in-law.

He was brooding and handsome in the lamplight, and as he gazed back at her she noticed a faint slackening of the lines of his mouth giving him a sensual look that was somehow intensified by the black velvet dinner-jacket he wore. Pryde, unlike Lucan, was a bit of a dandy. Her smile deepened, and in her beryl-coloured dress she was slim and decorative against the glossy frame of the piano. 'I have a favourite,' he said. 'It is Beethoven's *Appassionata,* but I think it would be too strong for your—small hands.'

'My hands have played most musical instruments, from a Greek lyre to a Spanish guitar.' She thought of her old passion for music and the many musical instruments that had cluttered her room when she had lived in the old family mansion at Andelos. 'My mother was English, so I was taught the piano as a child.'

She faced the keyboard and her fingers were mobile on the keys. Gently, with increasing feeling, the lovely music filled the room. She did not look up as Lucan came to sit in the shadows nearby, but she was aware all the time of his eyes upon her. What was he thinking? Her hands crashed out the chords of passion. What was he plotting? Alive and tempestuous, the music flowed from beneath her supple Greek hands, then the passion died away and sadness crept in. Twice she had loved, and each man in his own way had betrayed her trust in him. Her foolish, girlish, innocent trust.

Her hands crashed down on the keyboard and the *Appassionata* was ended.

'My dear,' Clare was all admiration, 'I had no idea you could play the piano so well.'

'I have always loved music.' Kara could feel herself trembling slightly from the reaction of her playing and her thoughts. 'I play with emotion, but any good music master would condemn my technique. I am sure

Pryde will tell you that I took liberties with the score.'

'You may take any liberties you wish, Kara,' he said gallantly.

'You are kind, Pryde.' She rose from the piano stool and went and sat in a chair near his. She did it with bravado, leaving Lucan alone in the shadows. Pryde opened the cigar box at his elbow, but Nils preferred a Black Prince and offered one to Lucan. Kara leaned back against a red cushion and watched Pryde's long, strong fingers on his cigar, squeezing gently so that the silky brown cylinder gave a crackle. He lighted it, and the dragon seal of his ring caught the lamplight and the tiny rubies blinked like eyes.

After the intensity of the music there was a sudden lull in the conversation, and the sound of the sea could be heard battering the cliffs below the terrace.

'When do you expect your land erosion expert?' Clare asked Lucan. 'Do you really think the old house is beginning to crack up?'

'I think it advisable to have the foundations checked, and the man I've written to should be here in a few days.' Lucan drew on his cigarette and his eyes narrowed through the smoke. 'The sea has a hungry sound these days. Have you noticed?'

Clare gave a visible shiver and pointed a brocade slipper at the fire. Always a fire was lit in the *salon* of an evening. Pryde felt the cold, and it grew strangely cold in this house at the edge of the sea when night fell.

'It occurs to me that each one of us in this room has an affinity with the sea.' Clare gazed around the hushed circle. 'We Savidges are here because the sea took a ship and tossed our ancestors on to these shores. Kara was born on an island in the Ionian, and Nils has the blood of Viking sea rovers in his veins. Perhaps that is why we listen to the voice of the sea and it seems to speak to us.'

'You have the imagination of the Irish and the artistic,' Nils said with a smile. 'The sea, like love, can be as kind as it can be cruel.'

'Love?' she cried. 'Why bring love into this?'

'Try keeping love out of anything,' he rejoined.

Clare frowned at him, and then took into her hands an ornament that always stood on the mantelpiece. A dappled fawn arrowed through the heart, whose outlines she traced with her sculptor's hands. 'I sometimes think that I would like to go and live in a thatched house in an Irish glen,' she said. 'But Dragon Bay holds too tightly to those born here.'

'Won't you go away when you marry?' asked Nils.

It seemed to Kara that he was provoking Clare to a quarrel; trying to shake her out of her coolness into a passion of some sort. For a moment the fawn trembled in her hand, then she replaced it very carefully and walked towards the double doors. There she stood for a moment, tall, graceful, tawny-haired, made to be loved yet denying herself to a man who, Kara was sure, could have made her happy.

'Nils, don't look at me like that,' she said with a laugh, 'as if you were trying to shatter me.'

'You cannot be melted, Clare,' he said, his eyes glacier blue. 'You are like the ice princess, and I wonder what it will take to shatter you. You know, Clare, there are volcanoes under ice in the far north. When they erupt the flame turns the ice to water—it runs away like a flood of tears.'

'I never weep, Nils. I leave that to the women who are foolish enough to love a man.' She swept him a mocking bow. 'Goodnight, Sweet Prince.'

The doors closed behind her, and after a restless hesitation Nils said goodnight himself and went out through the veranda doors. His footfalls rang on the steps and faded away

253

into the moonlight, among the trees.

Lucan tossed the end of his cigarette into the fire. 'The Savidges have a gift for hurting people,' he said, and the whip scar on his cheekbone seemed to stand out and catch Kara's eye. 'And we do it with style. "Goodnight, Sweet Prince." Horatio's last words to Hamlet, Prince of Denmark.'

'Poor Kara,' Pryde was looking at her. 'You must find us a bewildering clan, half devilish, half fascinating, eh? Like most of the Irish.'

'I—I try to understand you,' she said helplessly. 'I am Greek and we react with the heart, we don't fight with it.'

She stood up, slender, lost, caught like Nils in the cross-currents of tension that flowed among the Savidges. She glanced around her, as though seeking a rock to which she could cling, and her glance fell on the chessmen on a nearby table.

'I will leave you men to your game of chess,' she said. 'Who has the black knight in check?'

Lucan stood tall in the lamplight, his brows drawn down like a visor over his eyes, which held a flicker of steel.

'Lucan does appear to be checking my knight's progress to the queen.' Pryde lifted his cigar and he smiled faintly through the smoke. 'Are you going to try and vanquish me altogether, Lucan?'

Kara gave a shiver, for it seemed to her that there was a strange note of meaning in Pryde's remark. These twin brothers—once so close—were now combatants in an arena, and the arena was Dragon Bay.

> 'Cain, Cain . . .
> From earth to heaven vengeance cries,
> For thou hast brought thy brother down.'

Kara ran from the words to the double doors. Lucan with his long stride was ahead of her and opening them with sardonic courtesy. 'Goodnight, *seigneur*,' she threw a rather desperate glance at Pryde. 'Goodnight. . . .' She looked at her husband, but could not say his name. It seemed to catch in her throat, and gathering up her silken skirt she hastened across the hall to the great staircase, and the long mirrors gave back her golden reflection, here, there, a ghost who fled out of them and up the stairs of dark galleon timbers.

Upon reaching the Emerald Suite she looked in on Rue. The child was fast asleep, the night-lamp burning softly beside the bed,

255

and that red-plaited doll tucked beneath the covers beside her, its painted eyes staring in the half-light. Kara's hands clenched at her sides as she fought an impulse to snatch up the doll and throw it out of the window.

It made her think of black magic . . . of a cracked ceiling, of a wild scream, of a menace that stalked this house above the dragon-green bay.

She bent over Rue and kissed her russet hair. It smelled like wheat that had been in the sun all day, for Kara and the child had spent hours down on the sands. They both seemed happier away from the house, and Rue had said: 'I wish we could sleep in the beach house.'

Kara's face was pensive as she went into the adjoining room and closed the door quietly behind her. She opened the curtains, and the bright moonlight reminded her of the horse and rider she had seen the other night. They had not been ghosts but realities, and tonight in the *salon* Pryde had asked Lucan if he meant to vanquish him altogether.

Her fingers clenched on her silver worry beads. The desire for power did strange things to people . . . it unbalanced them, made them incapable of judging right from wrong.

Her gaze lifted to the moon, etched against

256

the dark sky like a golden shield with a corner chipped out of it. The moon waxed full, and someone at Dragon Bay was quite mad!

She tugged the curtains together and hurried over to switch on the bedside lamp, then obeying a sudden impulse she turned the key in the lock of the door that gave on to the gallery. No one could enter the suite with this door locked!

She prepared for bed, and after slipping beneath the covers read again the letter she had found awaiting her on the hall table that afternoon.

It was from her brother. Paul asked her to forgive him for his attitude towards her marriage. He was old-fashioned, and had not realized that Kara was a woman grown, with a mind and a heart of her own. He had hoped that she would find love with a young man of Greece, but he was happy if Lucan Savidge made her happy—

Kara fought back her tears by pummelling the pillows that felt as hard tonight as the stones upon which Jacob had laid his head.

The letter held loving messages from Domini, and from the small, curly-haired boy who wanted to know when Tante Kara was coming home. Oh, how delightful it would have been to see Rue and Dominic together!

She bit her lip painfully hard, for Paul wrote that she must bring her husband to Andelos as soon as possible, and they would celebrate her marriage in true Greek style. There would be lamb stuffed with herbs and roasted over an open fire, curd and honey tarts as big as wheels—the wine and the music would flow.

At the close of his letter, Paul asked again if she was truly happy. Was Lucan Savidge good to her? She had a large heart, Paul wrote simply, and only a big man would fill it.

Her heart lifted on a sigh. One hint to Paul that she was unhappy and afraid, and he would catch a plane to the Isle de Luc and take her away from Dragon Bay to the safety and security of his home on the island of Andelos.

She refolded his letter with a thoughtful expression, and was about to turn out the night-lamp when her gaze was caught by a movement of the door handle. It turned to the right, then to the left, then a voice spoke against the panels. 'I know you are awake, Kara, I can see the light beneath the door. May I come in and talk to you?'

Kara hesitated, feeling that she had borne all she could for one evening of the Savidge temperament. Then with a sigh she slid out of bed and shrugged into her robe. She turned the key in the lock and opened the door, and Clare stood looking at her with inquiring eyes. 'I—I know it's late,' she said in some agitation, 'but I had to talk to someone or go out of my mind.'

'Please come in.' Kara noticed with concern that Clare, her make-up removed and clad in a long silk dressing-robe, was unusually pale with shadows haunting her eyes. She sank down in a basket chair and as Kara closed the door she saw a tremor shake Clare from head to foot.

'I will switch on the electric fire.' Kara was glad herself of the glow of the bar and the warmth. She sat on the foot of the divan and studied Clare, who huddled forward, her long-fingered hands stretched to the fire.

'I was going crazy all alone in my room, listening to the sea. That damnable pounding, it gets into your head. "No peace for you. No peace for the wicked," it seems to keep drumming. Do you hear it, Kara? Does it worry you?'

Kara stared at Clare and felt the pounding of her heart, and the distant pounding of the waves. 'Why do you stay here, Clare? Anyone can see you are not happy, and you said the other day that your work was not going well.'

'Why do any of us stay?' Clare asked moodily. 'Why do you stay, Kara? You lock your bedroom door, against Lucan I presume?'

Kara caught her breath, lost for an excuse to offer his sister.

'So soon?' Clare said cynically. 'Has the gilt worn off the wedding vows? I have thought for days that you have looked unhappy, my dear, and I had such hopes that Lucan would settle down and be a good husband to you. You are like a deep-running brook, Kara, quiet on the surface but with undercurrents. Lucan needs those—he needs passion.'

Kara put her hands up against her cheeks and remembered his urgent arms and his kisses. If only love was all that Lucan needed, wanted—but he wanted what it was beyond her to give.

'One tries,' she whispered. 'I tried—hoped to make him care, but other things stand between us.'

'Caprice being one of them?' Clare said.

Kara nodded, her feet curled beneath her, her eyes big and dark in her pointed face. 'He told me of his trip to Paris, and his intention of proposing marriage to her. For some reason he left without asking her to be his wife—and then at Fort Fernand he met me

260

and—'

'You fell in love with him.' Clare spoke the words over which Kara hesitated.

'What is love?' Kara asked in bewilderment. 'I ran away from the Greek island where everyone knew I loved a young man named Nikos. I thought it love, and found it was something less. Nikos and I were dear companions, with no danger or excitement to learn from each other. I know that now, but at the time I was so blind to it. So very young.'

'Yes, young,' Clare echoed, the firelight gleaming on her tawny hair, gathered back from her temples, and her long neck. A lovely neck, showing through the opening of her silk robe the Venus crease which is said to denote a woman of strong passions. Yet Clare vowed she was cool, even heartless.

Their glances met and held, and Kara saw not coolness but anguish in Clare's grey eyes.

'What is wrong?' Kara asked. 'Do you care about hurting Nils?'

'Perhaps.' Clare rose to her feet and the silk robe sculptured the long, lovely lines of her figure. Her gaze dwelt on the door that separated this room from the one in which Rue was sleeping. 'Is she fast asleep?' Clare asked.

Kara nodded.

'May I—take a little peep at her?' Clare looked strange, and curiously eager. 'I am not sentimental about sleeping children, Kara, but I—I have a sudden longing to look at Rue while she sleeps.'

'Be very quiet,' Kara said, carefully opening the door of the big bedroom. Clare stepped in ahead of her and walked with care to the bedside. She stood looking down at the child, and then suddenly her hand was against her mouth and Kara heard a strangled sob as Clare hastened past her, into the other room again, where she sank down on her knees and buried her face in the cushion of the basket chair. She was weeping as Kara closed the door of Rue's room and leaned her shoulders against the panels.

'She's mine,' Clare sobbed. 'My child—my Rue.'

CHAPTER ELEVEN

THE heart-stricken sounds of Clare's weeping filled the room, and Kara hastened to her side and did what she could to ease this breaking down of the dam in Clare. This melting of the ice.

'It's true,' Clare gasped, seated at last in the chair, beaten, exhausted after her storm of tears. Her hair had loosened from its nape knot and hung to her shoulders. 'I couldn't go on any longer without telling someone. For years I have hated the very thought of Rue being mine. I—I have never admitted being her mother even to Lucan, but he knows. He has given her the love I should have given. He has taken the blame for her birth.'

Clare reached out and her hands clung to Kara's. 'I had to tell you because you must often have thought he was irresponsible, a heartless rake who made love to girls and did not care about the consequences.'

'Rue is eight years old,' Kara said in a shocked voice. 'For all that time you have let people believe a lie about your brother.'

'Yes.' Clare looked crushed, and the shadows beneath her wet eyes looked like bruises.

'Rue always looked so much like him, right from her birth. She had those green eyes, that russet hair, the smile that wrenched at you with its devilment. It was that devilment in Lucan, that streak of damn-you-all, think me Cain or the devil himself, that made the deception a sure one. I knew that Lucan would never betray me.'

Clare's eyes filled with tears that hung in her eyes. 'As the years went by I don't think he wanted people to think anything else but that Rue was his. He loves her, and she adores him. Sometimes I think this makes Pryde a little envious, but children are like little animals; they don't understand infirmity of the body.'

'Has Pryde never suspected the real truth?' Kara asked.

'Pryde believes what everyone else believes, that Lucan is Rue's father. He knows, as everyone else knows, that right from a boy Lucan had something about him that girls were irresistibly drawn to, like pins to a magnet. There were girls, of course, whose hearts he played around with, but I don't think he ever broke one.'

Kara tautened when Clare said that, for what of *her* heart, her feelings—her body which he had hurt in the cane, and possessed at the beach house with a totality that had left no room for a moment's tenderness?

'You look at me with such big and inquiring eyes,' Clare said with a sad smile. 'Your face is all expression, Kara. In the strangest way you are one of the loveliest people I have ever seen. Your eyes are so alive. They reflect a candour I truly envy. They are full of heart.'

Their glances held and Kara knew that at last she was looking at the real Clare, a woman with a tempestuous heart which she had concealed for years behind a mask of self-sufficiency.

'Yes,' Clare murmured, as if reading her thoughts, 'we all wear masks one way or another. When we have been hurt we need a mask to hide our scars, to conceal the secret passion we are ashamed of.'

'There can be no shame if the heart is involved,' Kara said. 'Did you not love the man—Rue's father?'

An expression of sheer pain tore at Clare's features. Her hands gripped Kara's until her nails stabbed. 'I shall never love another man as I loved Rue's father. He was handsome, utterly fascinating,' she said in a tortured voice. 'He was an expressionist painter whom I met in Paris when I went there to study art and sculpture. We would go to a café, argue and

265

eat paprika chicken. I knew he was a man to beware of, and yet I could not stay away from him. One evening he said that he had a friend who had a hunting lodge in a forest just outside Paris. He asked me to spend a week there with him.'

Clare paused in her recital and drew a deep sigh. 'I was eighteen and utterly at the mercy of his fascination. I was deeply in love and saw no wrong in giving in to that love. He was an artist, making his way as I was making mine, and I did not expect him to marry me.

'We went to the hunting lodge, a hidden away place of secret luxury, where the deer and the chamois were our only companions. We explored the woods. We talked and loved away the hours—and then one day a woman came to the lodge on horseback. She was about forty, with a face that might have been lovely before cynicism and high living had got at it. I was alone for an hour at the lodge, for Léon had gone off to swim in a nearby stream. I never cared for the water, and so I was alone when this woman appeared.

'"I own this place," she said to me. "The chateau whose turrets you see above the tree-tops belongs to me. Everything in this forest belongs to me—including the man who has been your lover for the past week. Léon is my husband."

'She swung the horse around and galloped away towards those distant turrets, and the day went grey for me. I stood there, Kara, shocked and horrified. I had never thought of Léon as a married man. I suppose in my foolish, romantic heart I hoped to make him love me so much that he would never let me go. When he returned from his swim I told him that I had met his wife. He smiled and shrugged his shoulders, took out a cigarette and lit it very casually. Yes, he was married. The lodge belonged to his wife, who was rich. He said he would never divorce her, and she would never divorce him. They understood each other. She wanted a young and handsome husband. He wanted a wealthy wife who permitted him the licence of his whims. To be an artist until the novelty wore off. To be the lover of young and pretty girls—until their attraction palled.

'I was appalled, Kara. I ran sobbing wildly through the woods, my pride utterly humiliated, knowing that I had given myself to a man to whom adulation was meat and drink. A man who cared nothing about me as a person, to whom I had been but a whim, another conquest, a passing pleasure.

'I returned to Paris, where I shared a flat

267

with Caprice. She was an artist's model who had become a fashion model, and whenever Lucan was in Paris on business he took Caprice out to dine and dance. I knew Nils even then, and I might have forgotten Léon in time—if that stolen week with him had not left me with a memento I could not run away from.

'I pretended I was going to Haiti to study Haitian sculpture. Instead I went to Trinidad and I lived there very quietly until Rue was born. No one knew I was a Savidge, for I lodged with a young Creole woman who ran my errands and I went out only in the evenings. She was a nice creature, poor but clever with her needle, and I gave her enough money to open a dressmaking shop—in return she had to take passage on a banana boat to the Isle de Luc, and then travel by road to Dragon Bay. When she reached the Bay she was to leave the child on the doorstep of the Great House—'

A shudder ran through Kara. How, she wondered, could Clare have done such a thing?

'It wasn't a total abandonment,' Clare said defensively. 'I knew Pryde would take her in. I knew he would take one look at Rue and know her for a Savidge—'

'And blame Lucan for her birth,' Kara broke in.

'Yes,' Clara admitted. 'No one could blame Pryde, and everyone could see that she had Lucan's green eyes and dark red hair. Everyone also knew that I was in Haiti. I flew there as soon as Marthe boarded that banana boat with Rue in her arms. Marthe could be trusted, and she has never broken my trust in her. She did all I asked of her, even to leaving a little note with the name Rue on it. When I returned at last to Dragon Bay, Rue was five years old. I was afraid to see her in case I saw Léon in her, but in all respects she is a Savidge—with, perhaps, the deer and the chamois in her from that week of heaven that ended in such disillusion that for years I have not been able to bear a man to touch me. It is only lately—'

There she broke off and sat looking in a lost way at Kara. 'How can I ever trust a man again?'

'How long,' Kara asked, 'have you known Nils Ericsson?'

'Why, since before Rue was born.'

'Then if it is Nils you are talking about, Clare, I would hardly say that he wants you for one week only.'

'I—I have put men out of my emotional

269

life,' Clare said rather desperately. 'I devote myself to my work.'

'To cold stone that can give you nothing but an ascetic satisfaction. Life for most people is unendurable without love, and you are not a born solitary, Clare. A person devoid of human needs.'

'Love involves you so, makes you so dependent on another human being. You know I am right, Kara. A woman's happiness is made or marred by the man she loves—if she is a real woman and not just a creature who can go from man to man and make a merry-go-round of life.'

'An ancient Greek once said that the price of every joy is a certain quota of pain.' Kara forced a smile to her lips. 'It is never easy to be a woman, Clare, but unless we let ourselves be women, foolish sometimes and romantic, hurt by so many things that could never hurt a man, then we are not really living. We merely go through the motions of living.'

'A woman alone is a deserted temple, full of the echoes of her dreams,' Clare said quietly. 'Nils is kind, but I feel none of the recklessness, the wild joy that I felt in Léon's company.'

'You were a young girl,' Kara pointed out. 'For a kind love, Clare, many women would

270

give their souls.'

'*You*, Kara?' Clare stared at her. 'Of course, I have been so wrapped up in my own misery that I have not spared a thought for you. My dear, Lucan's love could never be gentle. You must have known that from the first moment you met him.'

'Of course.' Kara lowered her eyes. 'I cannot expect Lucan to change—but, Clare, did it never occur to any of you that being thought a devil might have turned him into one?'

'He is a Savidge,' Clare said. 'We are a wild and self-willed clan, but our misdeeds have never been calculated. Kara, you can't expect him to be a saint. If you wanted that—'

'No, not a saint, but a man I could trust,' Kara said, and she seemed to hear again the thud of hooves through the cane, but now the face of the rider was known to her and she knew herself in deadly danger from that rider.

A tremor ran through her, and Clare said with sudden contrition. 'You must be tired, and I have kept you talking. Kara, I am so grateful for the way you have looked after Rue. I must seem to you the most unnatural mother on earth, and you are probably thinking that I should tell Rue that I am her mother. But I can't, Kara! And what we have

271

talked about tonight must remain a secret. You do understand?'

Kara shook her head. 'Not really.'

'Rue thinks of Lucan as her father. She loves him as she could never love me—it would not be a kindness but a cruelty to take her away from him. You see,' Clare rose to her feet and there was a sudden look of longing in her eyes, 'I want to go away from Dragon Bay. I think I want to go with Nils— to Denmark, perhaps, where we could start a new life together.'

'Rue is *your* child. How can you think of leaving her behind?'

'I can't take Léon's child into my life with Nils.' Clare walked quickly to the door. 'Nor can I break her little heart by taking her away from Lucan. Rue trusts him even if you don't!'

The door closed behind Clare, and Kara was left alone in the lamp shadows. *Trust is another name for love*, she thought bleakly. *All I am sure of is that tomorrow, or the day after, there will come a moment when I am alone—entirely alone with Lucan—and I shall wonder why I did not run a thousand miles from this house at Dragon Bay.*

*   *   *

There was to be a silver wedding party, and most of the workers on the Great House estate, including those who served in the house, had permission from Pryde to attend the festivities.

According to the young maid who attended to the Emerald Suite, the party was to be the gayest affair that Dragon Bay folks had known for a long time. There was to be a steel band, tables spread with goodies, and lots of dancing.

Rue danced with excitement and asked Kara to take her to see the 'silver bride'.

Clare was just entering the suite and she smiled as she caught Rue's remark. 'It would be fun,' she said. 'I know Lila and Bajo, the couple who are celebrating their twenty-five years together, and I am sure they wouldn't mind if I took Rue along to see the dancing. Would you like to go with me, Rue?'

Kara held her breath, and then Rue dashed across to Clare and hugged her around the waist.

Clare bit her lip, and then looked at Kara. A silent, eloquent look.

Kara could have gone to the party as well, but she wanted Rue to be alone with Clare and Nils. She hoped fervently that Clare would have the heart and the courage to tell the child that they were mother and daughter.

The date of the silver wedding dawned—a hot, still Friday that grew strangely silent when after lunch the servants trooped off in their bright dresses and smart suits, and Clare's small car turned out of the driveway, with Rue wriggling round in her seat to wave at Kara.

When the car was out of sight, Kara went back into the house. Through the silence that hung over the hall she heard the rustling of the miles of cane, grown tall and vividly green. Lucan was out there somewhere. He had been gone since early that morning, and he would return about four o'clock.

Her gaze dwelt on the door of Pryde's study. She took a step or two in that direction, and then she stood hesitant and her gaze was drawn upward to the ceiling, to the blank space where a chandelier had once glittered. Her heart gave a curious lurch, for the new white plaster was cracked right across, a dark wavering line that extended to the centre of the ceiling.

Her nerves tightened as the clock chimed three times, and then a cloud rolled across the sun and the hall darkened. Kara looked around her and saw her slim, nervous figure reflected in the panelled mirrors, one of which gave back her reflection in an oddly distorted way. She approached the mirror and saw that like the ceiling it was cracked all the way across.

Kara went cold. A cracked mirror was a bad omen, and even as she stared at her distorted reflection she heard a horse gallop into the stableyard at the rear of the house. Something prompted her to run to the door of Pryde's study. She pulled the door open. 'Pryde?' There was no answer, the room was empty of all but its rare ornaments, the lovely paintings and glossy crystal.

She gazed around her, and then crossed hastily to the window and glanced out. There was the stableyard, and a man dismounting from the back of a golden stallion with a lack of resilience that made her hand clench on the curtain. He walked in a halting way across the flagstones and entered the house through a side door. For seconds Kara couldn't move—she knew herself alone in the house with a man who was determined and dangerous, and quite without mercy.

She was halfway to the door when it was blocked by a figure in knee-boots and breeches, a white shirt and tilted field hat. And in that moment there was not a stirring of a leaf or a stalk of cane. That cloud over the

275

sun had not moved, yet the heat was tangible, weighing down all sound, pressing on the heart and the nerves.

The man and the girl stared at each other, then he swept off his hat and gave her a mocking bow.

'Pryde,' she whispered, and her pallor intensified the darkness of her eyes.

'Yes, my dear.' He took a heavy step into the room. 'Pryde the fallen, who walks again, and rides. Perhaps not with the grace of my devastatingly attractive brother, but then I never had his grace of body, his ability to charm, or his way with the workers.'

Kara could feel herself shaking—she clutched at the edge of the desk and it was as though the very earth shook beneath her. 'How long have you been able to walk—to ride?' Her voice shook as well.

'About a year ago I had a small accident,' he tossed the field hat to his desk. 'My wheelchair overturned and instead of finding myself a helpless object on the floor, I discovered to my joy that I could move my legs. Nils, such a very good masseur, has unknowingly been helping to restore the strength and flexibility to the lower half of my body. I am no longer helpless. I am again the complete master of Dragon Bay.'

276

'Why did you never say?' Kara's fear was giving way to fury. 'Why did you go on tormenting Lucan, playing the martyr, demanding his very soul for your loss of activity—no longer a loss but a recovery he would have rejoiced in?'

'For years Lucan has had the use of his body while I have been helpless in a wheelchair.' The grey eyes gleamed coldly, the handsome but sombre face was suddenly the face of a devil. 'I wanted him to suffer in all ways for that. I even hoped that at my prompting he would marry that pretty fool in Paris. She would have demanded his attention when he was needed about the plantations; she would have refused to spoil her model's figure by giving him the child that *I* demanded.'

Pryde gave a laugh, and poured himself a brandy from the decanter on his desk. 'Lucan looks so self-sufficient, eh?' He took a sip of the brandy and his eyes were fixed upon Kara. 'As though love—and I don't refer in this instance to physical love—were not a necessity he craves with all his secret, sentimental heart. He was always sentimental, and ashamed of showing it. Our mother preferred me because I had her ways, Lucan our father's. There was none of that Irish roman-

277

ticism in her. She revelled in being mistress of Dragon Bay, loved the power it gives to have a Great House and plantations filled with busy workers. Lucan looks upon it as a social obligation to provide as much work and as much comfort as possible for the people we employ.' Pryde laughed again, scornfully.

'Like the Irish brothers who founded Dragon Bay he would never make a slave of anyone—but I made a slave of him.'

Kara shuddered, and the ground beneath her feet seemed to shudder with her. 'It was you I saw the other night on that horse out there,' she said. 'It was you who rode me down in the cane.'

'What a pity you have discovered my secret,' he mocked. 'I meant you to think Lucan the culprit. I thought to change your heart, my dear. You are an unusual person, with a capacity for appreciating beauty, a woman of compassionate passion. I saw no reason why Lucan should have you.' He put down the wine glass and took a step towards Kara. 'I have a fancy for you myself.'

Her eyes grew wide with horror—if she tried to dart past him he would grab at her with those arms, made powerful by years of propelling a wheelchair. She glanced round wildly for a way to elude him, and then remembered that Lucan would be returning to the house at four o'clock. She must keep Pryde talking! She must keep on asking questions that he could not resist answering.

'You challenged Lucan to that climb up the cliffside,' she said. 'Did you hope that he would fall?'

'My dear, the Savidge dragon guards his own, don't you know that?' A gleam of admiration came into Pryde's eyes as he studied her. 'You are terribly afraid of me, yet you won't scream or attempt to run. You stand there defying me as the Sabine women must have defied their invaders.'

She looked at him, at the high nose and the cruel grey eyes, and she knew that at all costs she must not get anywhere near his arms.

'Da told your mother that Lucan was to blame for your fall—does she know that you can walk again?'

'Of course.' A smile flickered on his lips. 'Da has always been devoted to me. She does whatever I tell her, and when I knew I could ride again, her son bought me another Satan. The original Satan was sold off the island for stud purposes—and because everyone thought I would never ride again. Or love a woman again.'

Again he took a step nearer to Kara, and

279

she almost screamed aloud as beyond the windows something growled—thunder in the oppressive air—a flicker of lightning.

'I have seen more beautiful women that you, Kara, but none that had your strange, dark-eyed attraction. Your eyes are Byzantine—like that priceless vase over there.'

Kara followed the direction of his gesture to the Persian blue vase, glowing and lovely and irreplaceable. It stood on a stand to the left of Kara, and quick as lightning she darted to it, seized hold of the vase and dashed it to pieces in the fireplace. Pryde stared unbelievingly, then with an enraged cry he lumbered to the fireplace where the pieces of precious china were scattered. Kara then took her chance and fled past him, out of the door, into the hall, fear lending wings to her heels as she raced across to the front door.

'Da,' he bellowed behind her. 'Where are you you old witch? Don't let her get away!'

Kara fumbled with the front door and dragged it open, half aware that a dark figure was hastening down the great staircase. But Da was elderly, Kara was young and desperate. She ran down the wide steps of the veranda and across to the gateway that led into the cane fields. Lucan would come this way. Lucan. Lucan. Her heart pounded his name, and her lips made a silent prayer of it.

'*Lucan!*' She cried out his name and ran through the cane to the horseman who was galloping towards her. The cane stood tall, petrified by the heat. The cicadas shrilled, and then as if in a dream Kara was being lifted bodily on to the horse and strong arms were holding her shaking body close to a hard, warm chest.

Her hands clenched his shoulders, her whole being trembled with reaction, and the sudden overwhelming joy of being close to him, safe with him. And then she heard him say: 'My God, that's Pryde by the gateway!'

She turned her face from his shoulder to look, and then as Lucan cantered his horse towards the gateway, Pryde started back towards the house. There was a flicker of lightning and Lucan's horse gave an uneasy nicker and stood his ground just inside the gateway. The thunder growled, and they saw a tall figure outlined clearly against the veranda pillars, silent and unmoving, looking over towards them.

'Pryde!' Lucan cried, and the rest was drowned as the house trembled—like a reflection in a pool shattered by a stone—and the walls caved in, the tall chimneys fell, and the entire cliffside gave way and carried the

Great House with it.

With a roar like a great wounded beast the house was gone—the sea had taken it—nothing was left but a gaping maw into which the rain suddenly pelted.

'Dragon that loved this world and
held us to it,
You are broken, you are broken.'

Lucan turned his horse from the sight and they galloped until they came in sight of the overseer's house. Lucan dismounted and then reached for Kara and carried her in his arms into the porch. They stood there, arms tight around each other, clinging like shocked children to the warmth and aliveness of each other.

'I have to go back there,' Lucan said at last. 'Stay here, Kara—you'll be safe here.'

'Lucan—' She wanted to hold him, but knew she had to let him go and do what had to be done. He rode away again, to muster help and to search the wreckage on the beach for signs of life.

Hours later Lucan returned to her, tired, soaking wet, with that in his eyes that told her Pryde was gone, out of their lives for ever. Pryde had called her compassionate, and that was what she felt as she sat watching Lucan at the overseer's table, showered and wearing some of Josh's clothes, making an effort to eat the meal Josh had prepared for him.

Over the years the unrelenting bitterness in Pryde had turned to hatred for Lucan, and in the end to madness.

She lowered her gaze from Lucan's tired face as tears swam in her eyes. The strength of her doubt of him had been as strong as her love for him—she had stayed in the house that afternoon believing it was Lucan who sought to hurt her, and she would have died at his hands rather than live without him. She had known for days that she could not live without him. Separation, wide seas, days and nights without him would not have killed the love she felt for him.

Later they sat out on the porch in the starlit stillness. The rain had ceased, the sky had cieared, and somewhere among the trees a bird dropped its notes like pieces of silver.

Clare and the child, along with Nils, were staying at Lila's house. 'The sea took most of the Great House,' Lucan added. 'I hope Pryde didn't suffer.'

Kara sought her husband's hand and held it tightly, and after a while he asked her to tell him about that nightmare hour in Pryde's study. She hesitated, and he said that he had to know everything. She told him everything, and ended with her face buried deep against his chest.

'Did you really doubt my love, Kara?' His hand stroked her hair and there was a note of sadness in his voice.

'How could I know you loved me,' she whispered, 'when everything you said, everything you did seemed to be for Pryde's sake?'

'Could you not tell that I loved you that night at the beach house?' His lips were hard and warm against her temple. 'It was too deep for words what I felt. You were always so elusive, and I had waited too long to make you mine.'

'I thought even that was for Pryde's sake.' A tremor shook her voice. 'He was so unrelenting, Lucan, all those years. And he plotted to make me hate you—'

'I couldn't bear you to do that, Kara.'

'Lucan,' her fingers traced the strong bones of his face, felt the lines of secret pain beside his lips, 'why did you never say that you loved me?'

'You don't speak out loud about love at Dragon Bay,' he said.

'You can now, Lucan.' She pressed her lips very gently against the whip scar on his cheek. 'Try it, my dearest. Tell me that you care.'

'I'll do better than that.' There was a note of tender ferocity in his voice. He swept her close to his heart and the pain they had shared was eased by his kiss, and by the promise of happiness that could come now to Dragon Bay.

She clung to him, her lips warm with love. 'We will stay here and build again, Lucan,' she said in answer to his unspoken question. 'Too many people need you—and I need you most of all.'